Do-It-Yourself

Conflict Resolution for Couples

Dynamic New Ways for Couples to Heal Their Own Relationships

By

Florence Bienenfeld, Ph.D., M.F.C.C.

CAREER PRESS
Franklin Lakes, NJ

DO-IT-YOURSELF CONFLICT RESOLUTION FOR COUPLES
Cover design by Cheryl Finbow
Typesetting by Eileen Munson
Printed in the U.S.A. by Book-mart Press

To order this title, please call toll-free 1-800-CAREER-1 (NJ and Canada: 201-848-0310) to order using VISA or MasterCard, or for further information on books from Career Press.

The Career Press, Inc., 3 Tice Road, PO Box 687, Franklin Lakes, NJ 07417

Library of Congress Cataloging-in-Publication Data

Bienenfeld, Florence.
  Do-it-yourself conflict resolution for couples : dynamic new ways
for couples to heal their own relationships / by Florence
Bienenfeld.
    p. cm.
  Includes index.
  ISBN 1-56414-437-2
  1. Conflict management. 2. Couples. 3. Man-woman relationships.
  4. Interpersonal relations.   I. Title.
HM1126.B53   1999
303.6'9--dc21   99-41528

}{

To our newlyweds
Kimm and Joel
and
to all couples willing
to discover
new, dynamic ways
for resolving
conflicts and problems

}{

Acknowledgments

I wish to express my appreciation to Sheree Bykovsky, my literary agent, and the entire staff of Sheree Bykofsky and Associates, Inc., with special thanks to Janet Rosen; to my publisher, Ron Fry, President of Career Press, Stacey A. Farkas, Managing Editor, and the entire staff of Career Press; and to Pedro de Cordoba of Pedro's Word Processing.

A very special word of appreciation to Sheldon Kardener, M.D., Psychiatrist, Clinical Professor of Psychiatry, Department of Psychiatry and Biobehavioral Sciences, University of California at Los Angeles and in private practice in Santa Monica, California, for writing this enthusiastic Foreword.

I would like to express my gratitude to my counseling clients over a 30-year period for sharing their lives with me and educating me as I educated them.

Last, but not least, I wish to thank Mickey, my loving husband of, soon to be, 50 years, whose love, encouragement, and support makes everything possible; and our loving, talented children and grandchildren, all who bring me such warmth and joy.

Contents

Foreword

For more than 30 years, Dr. Florence Bienenfeld has worked with her clients in a variety of settings. These have varied from the County of Los Angeles Superior Court family mediation program to private practice to leading seminars on divorce and child custody. Through all of these venues, she has gained an enormous wealth of experience across a wide spectrum of human relationship difficulties. In this volume, she shares her experience, knowledge, understanding, and helpful perspective in a way that permits the reader to sit alongside her as she approaches the people she sees and the problems they present.

At the same time, there is something with which we all can identify to some degree in ourselves and our own significant relationships in the nature of the problems being presented by the clients. The carefully detailed expositions of the difficulties being experienced are matched with an equally clear and detailed discussion of the ways one can begin to become free of the turmoil created by the conflicts.

There is a very sensitive discussion of the nature of the difficulties, followed by good, clear, step-wise directions that can lead to a solution. It is in this way that we recognize how very much Dr. Bienenfeld is imparting to her clients and to us, the readers, who recognize ourselves in the struggles presented. She does so with the experienced gift of "what to do's" that addresses the issues and then leads to a resolution.

In even the most cursory look at the Contents, we see breadth and scope of the discussions that lie ahead. There is great pain being experienced in the suffering presented. There is great relief in the plan and program presented. In *Do-It-Yourself Conflict Resolution for Couples* are meaningful ways presented for people to deal with the obstacles that interfere with fulfilling relationships. But at the same time, the author stresses that there is a limit to the extent one can apply these solutions. Wisely, she points out that the "do-it-yourself" part applies when it can be followed, and is allowed to work. When it cannot, then clients are urged to seek therapy to help them come to the position that will allow these "templates for trouble" to be applied and from which great benefit can be derived. You are in for stimulating, valuable, and entirely practical and useful reading. Enjoy!

Sheldon Kardener, M.D.

Sheldon Kardener, M.D., Psychiatrist, is a Clinical Professor of Psychiatry, Department of Psychiatry and Biobehavioral Sciences, at University of California at Los Angeles and is in private practice in Santa Monica, California.

Introduction

Since 1968, I have been counseling couples. Even after all these years it still amazes me how differently two partners can perceive the same situation. This is because each partner sees everything that transpires between them through his or her own eyes and experience. As a result, even in the best of relationships, couples are bound to have differences and disagreements and are in need of effective skills for resolving them.

The cause of most breakups is the pressure from *unresolved* conflicts. Unresolved issues put couples at risk by weakening the bond between partners and eroding away their closeness, leaving both partners feeling frustrated, angry, and alone.

Do-It-Yourself Conflict Resolution for Couples is the first book to give couples practical and effective techniques for resolving their disagreements and communicating about sensitive issues. By mastering a repertoire of conflict resolution skills, couples can settle issues and problems as they arise, before they become festering sores that never heal. Once mastered, these valuable relationship skills can serve and benefit couples for a lifetime. Instead of feeling helpless and powerless, couples are empowered once their new, dynamic skills replace old, ineffective ways of dealing with problems.

Do-It-Yourself Conflict Resolution for Couples abounds in dynamic conflict resolution processes designed to help couples resolve disagreements, clear away resentments, express anger maturely, reduce tension and anxiety, handle problems, and heal troubled relationships. Each process provides couples with the necessary structure and support for resolving their problems and conflicts. The anecdotal case material throughout demonstrates the positive movement that these processes can bring about. In my counseling practice, I developed methods to help my clients transform their lives and their relationships. Throughout *Do-It-Yourself Conflict Resolution for Couples*, I will be sharing these methods with you. Actual case material is presented to demonstrate the effectiveness of my methods, although names are fictitious and other identifiable material has been changed or disguised to protect confidentiality.

Couples of all ages, married and unmarried, gay and straight, will benefit enormously from the insights and skills to be discovered and mastered in *Do-It-Yourself Conflict Resolution for Couples*.

As a marriage counselor for more than 30 years, and a family mediator for 10 of those years in the Conciliation Court of Los Angeles County Superior Court, I have counseled thousands of couples. Each couple would tell me their difficulties and all the suffering they were going through. When couples were willing to work on their relationships, I worked with them on resolving their conflicts and problems. But not all couples can afford or find private counselors or mediators to help them resolve their difficulties. It is for couples such as these that *Do-It-Yourself Conflict Resolution for Couples* is intended.

A word of caution: The dynamic processes for resolving conflict throughout *Do-It-Yourself Conflict Resolution for Couples* involve being willing to sit and listen to your partner even if his or her opinion is contrary to your own. This can be frustrating, and for people who have a low frustration tolerance, this can be extremely difficult. Chapter 2 can be very helpful, however, professional help should be sought by individuals or couples who are not able to listen to each other without exploding, becoming physically or verbally abusive, or very depressed.

Do-It-Yourself Conflict Resolution for Couples is designed to give couples new insights, support, and skills for making their relationships the best they can be. Once couples resolve problems and change certain conditions and behaviors that are tearing them apart, their relationships can be transformed. I have seen this happen over and over again.

I send all of you my encouragement and best wishes.

CHAPTER 1

Resolving Disagreements Amicably

Settling disagreements is difficult when both partners have strong feelings about the issues involved. Not uncommonly, egos are also involved, which can make resolution extremely difficult.

Jenny and Charley were having frequent disagreements and power struggles. Charley told why he thought this kept happening: "We're both stubborn and neither one of us will give in. Once we get an idea set in our minds, we're like bulls. We're both too proud to back down."

When partners disagree, what often happens is that both partners talk, or yell, at once, and no one listens. This causes frustration levels to rise. Partners say things in anger and a resolution of their disagreement is far out of reach.

My experience as a family mediator working at the courthouse with divorcing parents who were fighting over custody of their children taught me very quickly to structure the mediation sessions. Free-for-alls accomplished nothing. So when these parents would begin to argue, both talking at once, I would soon say, "I'm sure you could argue without me. I would like to find out how each of you sees the situation and then we can discuss the issues you raise. Who would like to go first?" One of the parents would begin or they would decide between them who would go first. Once one parent began, I did not allow the other parent to interrupt until the first parent had finished, at which time we switched and the other parent would have a turn. The structure I imposed on them gave each parent a turn to express his or her thoughts and feelings. Afterward, I would ask them each to take turns proposing a parenting plan and discussing the issues they each wished to resolve in the mediation session. On those issues that the parents disagreed, I asked them to explore various options for resolving their disputes.

Through give-and-take and compromise, more than 70 percent of these litigating parents were able to reach parenting agreements. This is truly amazing—from chaos to order and from despair to hope.

After my experience counseling and mediating for more than 10 years in the courthouse, I went back into private practice. I transposed what had worked with very angry, hostile divorcing parents to use in my counseling practice with couples, and reaped fine results. Because not all couples have the luxury or availability of a counselor or mediator, I developed the Five-Step Conflict Resolution Process for couples to do on their own.

Setting the mood for conflict resolution

Conflict resolution takes time and energy. This work should not be done when either partner is rushed, or overly tired, when other people are present, or children are running underfoot. It is preferable for both partners to mutually agree upon a time to get together.

Tact and skill are greatly advised when you approach your partner regarding discussing certain issues. Using "I" messages is the safest approach because "I" messages are not attacking. "I" messages begin with the word "I" and continue with a description of what you are feeling and what you want. For example, you might say, "*I* have been upset (or lonely, or frustrated, or worried, etc.) lately and *I* want to sit down with you to discuss what is bothering me. *I* want this to be a positive experience for both of us. After *I* tell you what is troubling me, then *I* am willing to listen to how you see this situation. After we each express ourselves, then, hopefully, we can work out a solution. *I* would like to arrange a convenient time for us to meet."

It is best to avoid "you" messages and "why" messages because they sound attacking and are likely to put your partner on the defensive. "You" and "why" messages might sound like this: "*You* make me so upset and miserable (or frustrated, or angry, or lonely, etc.). *Why* do you always do that? *You* better sit down with me and work this out or I'm going to give up on you." It is very easy to see how this could put someone on the defensive.

Meet at a place where you and your partner won't be disturbed for about two hours. If you can't find a quiet place, consider meeting in your car, parked away from your home. During the meeting, should tempers flare and threaten to get out of control, separate and take a short break with some slow, deep breaths until you both calm down. Then resume your meeting.

Instructions for five-step process

Before beginning this process, it is best that both partners read over the instructions once or twice, then follow the structure and format of the process exactly. During the conflict resolution meeting, partners should stick to the issues to be resolved and avoid "kitchen-sink" free-for-alls, which can ruin the chances for a positive outcome.

Step 1. Sit facing your partner and establish eye contact. This can be very difficult, especially when one or both partners are upset. Eye contact, though, helps to create a therapeutic, conciliatory atmosphere.

Step 2. Take turns with your partner telling how each of you sees the situation regarding the disputed issue or issues, including your concerns and feelings.

Either partner may begin first, using "I" messages. Once one begins, the other may not interrupt, even if you disagree with what your partner is saying or how your partner sees the situation. After your partner has finished, then take your turn and tell how you see the situation. Step 2 can be repeated once both partners have had a turn, if either partner has anything to add.

Step 3. Take turns with your partner exploring and proposing various alternatives for reaching a solution to your disagreement or dispute. Proposals should reflect solutions each partner is willing to consider. Step 3 can be repeated if either partner has anything to add.

Step 4. Take turns stating what you would each be willing to consider in order to settle your disagreement.

Step 5. When possible, work out an agreement through mutual give-and-take or compromise. This means you sometimes give in when something is really important to your partner, your partner gives in to you when something is very important to you, and sometimes both of you compromise to reach an agreement. This give-and-take allows both partners to feel good about the relationship. If only one partner continually has to give in, while the other partner always gets what he or she wants, the partner who is always giving eventually feels taken advantage of or unloved. This can lead to serious rifts between the two partners. Compromise is not always possible. At times it is necessary for one partner to give in on an issue, especially when it is very important to the other partner.

Contrary to what many people believe, giving in is not a sign of weakness, unless, of course, one's safety, self-respect, or integrity is at stake. Giving in and/or compromising to reach an agreement is actually a sign of strength and maturity, in addition to concern for resolution and love for the other person.

Five-Step Conflict Resolution Process

Linda and George were having a disagreement over whether to send their son, Johnny, to summer camp. Their discussion during the five-step process demonstrates the movement that is possible when couples are willing to discuss issues and listen to each other. In Step 1, Linda and George sit facing each other and establish eye contact. During Step 2 they tell each other how they perceive the issue being resolved.

Linda:

"I don't want to send Johnny to camp this year. I think he's still too young for sleep-away camp. Last year he cried every time we called him, and he begged us to come and get him. It broke my heart. It would make me feel very sad to send him there again. When he's older, we can send him."

George:

"I don't think he's too young. All his friends are going. If he doesn't go to camp, he'll have no one to play with, and he'll be bored. Besides, I want him to become more independent. He's already 9 years old, and he still hangs onto you like a baby. Camp will make him stronger and more independent. I don't want him to be a mama's boy. You've got to let go of him sometime!"

As you can see, during Step 2 both partners expressed deep feelings. Linda told George how tormented and torn apart she felt when their son was miserable at camp, and George shared his deep concern that their son grow to be more independent and not be permanently tied to his mother's apron strings. This communication was important and the feelings were real for each of them. Each had his or her own view of the situation. Their feelings were neither right nor wrong, and they could not help how they felt. Feelings should be heard and acknowledged even when we don't agree with them.

During Step 3, the couple take turns proposing various possible solutions; they reflect what each is willing to consider:

George:

"This year we could send Johnny to camp for only two weeks instead of a month."

Linda:

"Johnny could either go to a day-camp this summer, or a summer school program, or visit your parents. Then next year we can send him to sleep-away camp for sure."

The partners have each stated what he or she would consider for this year, and Linda even mentioned what she would consider for next year.

During Step 4 the partners state what each would be willing to accept in order to settle their disagreement:

George:

"I'll give in this year as long as you're promising to send him next year. I'd be willing for Johnny to go to sleep-away camp this year for only two weeks instead of a month, or this year he could go to day-camp, and then visit my parents for two weeks."

Linda:

"Thank you so much. I'm sorry. I just can't send him to sleep-away camp this year after what happened last year. But next year he will go for sure. I'd be willing for him to go to day-camp and visit your parents for two weeks this year."

George and Linda now have a basis for resolving their disagreement. During Step 5 they settled on sending Johnny to day-camp and for a visit with his grandparents for two weeks this year, thus avoiding prolonged tension between them.

This model for dispute resolution can work if both partners are willing to allow the other to express feelings without interrupting, and if both are willing to negotiate a settlement by mutual give-and-take and compromise. Couples who are unable to work out their problems on their own are wise to seek professional help as soon as possible before partners lose feelings for each other.

Janet and David resolve issues

When Janet and David received an offer on their house, David wanted to sell, but Janet felt it wasn't the right time for them to do so. Following is a transcription of this couple's use of the five-step process to settle their disagreement.

Step 1.   Janet and David sit facing each other and establish eye contact.

Step 2.   Janet and David take turns telling how they each perceive their disputed issue. Janet asks David to go first. David hesitates at first, then begins.

David:

"Where can I begin? Okay, I like our house. It's not like I hate our house. For 17 years you've been telling me that you hate living in Los Angeles and you want to move back to Ohio. All these years, you've been miserable being in Los Angeles. It's only fair for you to get your turn to decide where we live. I basically agree that I'm willing to try living some other place.

"I'm afraid if we don't sell, we'll miss a window of opportunity to sell our house. We have an offer now and the climate for selling could change. On the other hand, it could become great for sellers and if we sold now we could lose money. I have other considerations about selling, which are not so much about selling but about moving from Los Angeles. I will miss my family terribly and will have to start all over again with my work somewhere else. It's not easy, but I would do it. What I really want to do is try to live somewhere else. This would involve selling our house or renting it while we try living elsewhere.

"The other aspect is that, in the last several years, we've had this business together. I had a deep feeling that it was our business that was holding us together. I'm less convinced of this now than I was a month ago, since we went away alone together.

"I have felt for a long time that this is not a good house for us even though it's pretty. You and I have had a lot of problems. The idea of moving into another house, either buying or renting, and trying to live somewhere else wouldn't be unappealing to me." David nods to Janet to begin.

Janet:

"Well, this was prompted by getting an offer on the house. We put our house on the market. We got an offer right away, and I think this made it more real for us. I freaked out. I wouldn't want to be uprooted right now. Our house has been very difficult to live in. A lot of water problems, a lot of maintenance issues, which I take care of. But yet, it doesn't feel like the right time. My concern in accepting this offer is that I'm going to be the one to move us. I don't really want to go through that at this moment.

"Maybe in a few months, maybe in the summer. But I'm not clear where I want to move. I don't want to pick up all this stuff and move it into another house somewhere temporarily. It's completely unappealing to me. It would take us six months to get resettled. Then there's the thought of going someplace else. I don't want to move twice. So that's it. I'd like to get a clear plan of what we're going to be doing before we tell somebody we'll accept the offer. Also, we need to do a little more thinking about the kids. This is such a great location for them. Uprooting them will be hard. I don't know where we should move. Also I think that the market's going to go up. Kathy (their real estate agent) told me that our house will be very easy to sell. So if we pass on this offer, we would still be able to sell it to somebody else. You know this offer is low. We need to get more for the house."

Step 3. Janet and David move on to proposing alternatives for reaching a solution.

Janet:

"What I propose is that we call Kathy and tell her that we're just not ready to sell. I know you are planning to be gone in March and April for your training and I don't want to be in escrow, closing a property, when you're not here. I'm not willing to do that. So, when you are finished with your training in the middle of May, that will be a better time. The kids will be finished with school. We'll have a better idea where we want to move or places we want to check out. Things will be more settled with our business, and that will feel like an easier time to pack up. We can start accepting offers in June."

David:

"I wouldn't want to be in a position of having to move twice either. Better to know where we want to go, and then go there. It would be easier to wait till June to sell. That will give us some time to decide what we want to do. Of course, we could also keep doing what we're doing and not sell. That's an option, too."

Janet:

"I'm looking at this offer. It's too low. I'm looking at the comparables in our area." (Janet had brought in the offer and was glancing at it.)

David:

"This year we could rent our house out. You have to figure out if you want to move somewhere else or not. It seems clear to me. I think in this case I'm sold that we can't accept this offer and we need to raise the price of our house."

Janet:

"I think we have the same idea."

Step 4. Janet and David each state what they would be willing to consider.

David:

"What I would be willing to do is not accept this offer and put the house on the market in June. Then in the spring, you could go to Ohio and look around and decide for yourself if you really do want to move there."

Janet:

"You know, I think I'll be clearer by then. We may have to go look at more places or stay here to be close to your family. We'll see. We'll decline this offer and I'll make an exploratory trip to Ohio to look at the possibilities of moving there. By the time you return at the end of May, beginning of June, we will be clear by then what we want to do. Then, we can put the house on the market officially and know better what we want to do."

Step 5. Janet and David reach an agreement.

David:

"I agree."

Janet:

"Yeah, I think we'd be giving it away at this price. It's just way too low. Our house is really nice."

David:

"Right."

After they were finished with the five-step process, I asked Janet and David to describe how this process helped them. They agreed that the process helped to clarify things. David added, "It brought us together from a place where we were adversaries to a place where now we're working together as a team."

The five-step process for conflict resolution is designed to allow both partners to express themselves completely without interruption, to be heard by their partner, to think through a variety of alternatives, and to reach a mutually agreeable solution through give-and-take or compromise. This structural approach also gives couples a feeling of peacefulness and satisfaction, not frustration that is often felt after shouting matches.

So often, even when disagreements are discussed and appear settled, angry feelings persist or one or both partners feel that he or she was the one who gave in—and always have to give in. This creates tension in the relationship, which is bound to surface sooner or later in some way or other.

The great value of resolving disagreements amicably, using the format I have suggested in the Five-Step Conflict Resolution Process, is that, afterwards, both partners can feel like winners and both can feel good about themselves and each other, thus enhancing closeness and intimacy.

CHAPTER 2

Clearing
Away
Resentments

Suppose you feel angry or upset with that special person in your life and you have no trouble expressing your feelings to him or her. Afterward, you would probably feel less upset and closer to that person, right? But what if you can't talk to that person, or he or she won't listen to you? Your negative feelings probably wouldn't go away and your resentments would weigh even heavier on you.

I bring this up to point out that many couples find it very difficult to discuss feelings and sensitive issues, thus leading to serious rifts. The problem mentioned most often by the couples I counsel is the inability to talk things over. Some say they have given up trying to talk to one another altogether. Every time they try, their efforts end up as arguments or in the silent treatment. As a result, instead of growing closer, many couples grow distant.

This distance develops because hurt and angry feelings need to be expressed to our partner. Otherwise these negative feelings stay around and can become more and more intense. It is difficult to feel close to our partner when we can't express ourselves, because we feel uncared about and unloved. As time goes by, if this pattern continues, those warm, loving feelings we once had for our partner get buried under all the negative feelings we are holding inside. Eventually, we can barely feel that love anymore.

This is what happened to Ed and Rita who were still living together, but were thinking of separating. Ed described how he saw their problem: "I feel very frustrated because Rita won't talk to me when she's upset. She clams up. I can feel the distance and coldness growing between us. I feel hurt and rejected. When I try to get her to talk, she turns away, cries, and goes off to our room. What can I do?"

Rita told her side of the story. "I used to try to talk to Ed and tell him my feelings, but he never listened. Instead, he would get angry, interrupt me, and tell me how wrong I was for feeling the way I did. After awhile, I gave up trying. Now I keep my feelings to myself."

Rita and Ed became strangers instead of friends and partners. Their inability to communicate destroyed their feelings for each other. This chapter is designed to help couples avoid such needless distancing and destruction. The Face-to-Face Communication Process that follows is structured to allow each partner to express and clear away resentments and be heard by his or her partner. In situations where verbal communication is unwise, as in cases of domestic violence, I recommend two alternative processes: putting it in writing and taping your resentments.

The Face-to-Face Communication Process

In my counseling practice, I have helped many couples just like Ed and Rita clear away their resentments by using a structured communication process designed especially to help couples release frustrations, anger, hurt, and resentment. It is ideal for couples who have difficulty communicating.

Instructions for Face-to-Face Communication Process

During the first half of this process, couples share resentments, concerns, and regrets. This usually takes from one and one half to two hours. Ideally, the second half of the process should be done on another day, or, at the least, after a rest break of no less than one hour. Otherwise, partners are likely to become tired or drained because they share very emotional material. During the second half of the process, couples share their wants, needs, and what they are willing to do to make their relationship work. This second half takes about two hours.

In order to maximize the benefits of this process, instructions should be read by both partners and then followed carefully. Some couples prefer, or may actually need, the assistance of a counselor or therapist to lead them through the process. This is strongly recommended if there has been any history of physical violence between the partners. Couples who do this process on their own should set aside enough time to be alone, and should take as much time as needed to complete each part of the process. If time runs out or one partner or both become too tired, then the process can be continued at another time.

Part I. Sharing resentments

Turn chairs toward each other so you are face-to-face, and establish eye contact. Many partners find this hard to do, especially if they have been avoiding each other's eyes. Decide between yourselves who will go first. The partner who goes first becomes the speaker; the other, the listener. The listener must not interrupt, even if he or she disagrees with what the speaker is saying. (The listener might pretend to have tape over his or her mouth and be unable to speak.) The listener should do just that—listen to what is being said, while also being aware of his or her own feelings. When it is your turn to speak, use the words, "I resent," or "I resented," then complete the sentence, stating what you resent or resented. For example: "I resent the way you bully me." Continue sharing all of your resentments even if they have been expressed a thousand times before. This is your chance to get them all up, out, and over with. Resentments might be difficult for your partner to listen to. So, after this exercise, let go of these resentments and don't bring them up again. Resentments usually take the longest to share, because there are often so many of them.

Listening skills are as important as sharing. This process is structured so that the listener listens without interrupting. It is not until the first speaker has completely finished sharing all of her or his resentments that partners switch roles. When partners switch, the new speaker brings up his or her own resentments and should not respond to what the speaker has just said. The new speaker also should not attempt to defend himself or herself.

There's no need for rebuttals or need to respond to what the other person expressed. Remember, feelings are not right or wrong. They just are. Feelings can also change from moment to moment, and when feelings are expressed, then anger or hurt can disappear. It is when feelings stay bottled up inside that they persist, fester, and destroy relationships.

There is a great difference between feelings and actions. It's okay to feel any way you feel. It's *not* okay to act out all of those feelings. There is great power in being able to experience your feelings, and at the same time, being able to control your impulses and actions. You might feel like punching someone, but you don't have to do it. This is called impulse control. We all need to develop impulse control to be truly mature adults. Otherwise, we would all go around acting out our feelings like children.

Part II: Sharing concerns

During this part, share your concerns: what you are feeling tense, anxious, worried, or apprehensive about. Again, decide who will begin. Use the words, "I'm concerned," and then say what it is that concerns you. For example, "I'm concerned we're going to lose our house if we don't stop spending so much." Once all of one partner's concerns are expressed, the partners switch roles.

Part III: Sharing regrets

After concerns have been shared, decide who will first share regrets. Begin with the words, "I regret," and add all the things you regret, feel sorry or sad about, wish you had done differently, or wish you hadn't done at all. For instance: "I regret not talking to you sooner about what I'm feeling."

Part IV: Sharing what you want

Share what you each want to see happen in your relationship and in your life. Begin with the words, "I want," and then say what it is you want. For instance, "I want to be able to trust you."

Part V: Sharing what you need

During this part, say what you need and *must* have to make your relationship work for you. These may seem similar to "wants" but they are much stronger; these are bottom-line issues. Be honest and tell it like it really is. Begin with the words, "I need," or "I must have," then say what you need or must have in order for your relationship to work for you. For example: "I need a little time to myself, a few hours a week, and I need you to watch the kids for me."

Part VI: Sharing willingness to help

During this last part, share what you are willing to do or give to make your relationship work. Decide who will begin. Use the words, "I'm willing to," and add what you are willing to do. For example, "I'm willing to watch the kids on Saturday afternoon so you can have a few hours to yourself."

Six couples each sharing one part of the process

Terri and John share resentments

Terri and John were ready to separate when they decided to come in for counseling. They both agreed to work on communication during their second session with me. Terri, age 23, faced her boyfriend. She laughed nervously when they first established eye contact, but her jaw soon tightened as she got in touch with the anger and frustration that had been there for some time. She began to speak. "I resent the way you tune me out. I resent the way you don't share yourself with me. I know you have feelings, but you won't let them be there. I resent the way you won't give. I feel sorry for you. I resent your phoniness, the way you try to get attention from people and never let people know you. I resent your selfishness. I want to be part of your life."

After Terri finished, John began. "I resent the way you always have to be right and won't consider my feelings. I resent the way you try to mold me and don't accept me as I am, or consider my background. I do care for people. I resent that you think I'm selfish. I'm a very loving person, but I hold it more inside than you do. I'm less affectionate than you are. You kiss this one and that one. I'd like to be more affectionate like you want me to be, but that's not the way I am. The emotions are there. I'm a very emotional person. I'm soft-hearted and I love animals. I resent the way you don't respect my feelings. I become frustrated and uncomfortable. I'm afraid of what you'll say. I resent having to watch my actions. I resent your bringing up the past and putting me down and saying 'always' and 'never' and comparing me to your old boyfriend. I feel hurt when you do that."

Laura and Dennis share concerns

After sharing resentments, couples next share their concerns. The concerns are what each partner feels tense, anxious, worried, or apprehensive about.

Dennis looked wearily into Laura's eyes and began. "I'm concerned about not being recognized as an individual. I don't feel we can talk to each other as friends. I'm concerned about being unemployed and not finding a job that I like. I'm concerned about money. I'm concerned about maintaining our home and not dipping into savings. I'm concerned about the children, that they don't get spoiled. I'm concerned about your inconsistency, the way you lose your temper and self-control."

Laura listened actively. When Dennis finished, she began. "I'm concerned about not communicating the way you want me to, and the way it affects our sex life. I'm concerned about your being at home all the time and not looking for a job, and the way you blame it all on your age. I'm concerned about not doing things the way you want me to. And how you become impatient with me if I don't do things according to the way you want me to. I'm concerned you won't change, yet you expect me to."

Nancy and Roy share regrets

After concerns have been shared, I ask couples to share their regrets, using the words, "I regret," then adding all the things they regret, feel sorry or sad about, wish they had done differently, or wish they hadn't done at all. Apologies can help clear the air and help couples begin again. It's the opposite of being defensive and having to be right. If one partner can say, "I'm sorry," it gives the other partner the space to do the same.

Both men and women often cry when regrets are being shared. Some fight hard to hold back the tears. I encourage them to experience the sadness if it's there, and not push it down.

Nancy faced her husband, Roy. "I regret not finding help sooner. I've been depressed for so long. I regret withdrawing from you into my own shell. I regret keeping my feelings to myself and not telling you how sad and depressed I felt. I'm sorry I haven't been a decent wife to you. I'm sorry I stopped giving you love."

When Nancy finished, Roy began. "I have lots of regrets: using profane language to get my point across, being impatient and short-tempered with you, and being a first-class ass for causing you the grief that I have. I regret not being able to see through your problem and help you along." Tears began streaming down his face. "I feel so ashamed. Why couldn't we have done this ourselves? I didn't realize I put you down and made you feel like a second-class citizen. I regret I didn't pick up on your problem when your mother died. I'm sorry." With that, they both cried.

Usually resentments, concerns, and regrets are shared in about one and a half to two hours. This completes the first half of the Face-to-Face Communication Process. The material shared by couples during the first half of this process allows partners to express what has often been on their minds and in their hearts for a long time. Once this has been accomplished, I encourage partners to leave the past behind them.

Before beginning the second half of the process, I usually suggest that couples take a break and continue the second half at another time. With the past behind them, the focus of the second half is on the present and the future, on what partners want, need, and are willing to do to make their relationships work.

Sandra and Arthur share what each wants

Sandra told me she was shocked when her husband wanted to separate. "I knew things had been bad for a long time, but I never thought he would leave me. I realized that either I was going to stop yelling at him and start meeting some of his needs, or lose him."

Arthur told Sandra what he wanted to see happen now. "I want less rejection. I want to have friends. I want to be happy and feel our son's going to be happy. I want sex. I want to feel needed and to play an emotional role in your life. I want to be admired."

Now it was Sandra's chance to share what she wanted. She looked at Arthur intensely and began. "I want mostly tolerance for my smoking and my inability to get things done. I already have enough guilt about this. I want to be loved for how I am. I need acceptance, not how I could be or how I should be. This is the main thing I want. I do want to stop smoking, but I don't want to deal with this now."

Jan and Dan share what each needs

Next, partners share needs—what they each *must* have to make their relationship work for them. These may seem similar to "wants," but they are much stronger. These are bottom-line issues.

Jan looked into Dan's eyes searchingly. They married three years ago, have two small children, and were seriously considering divorce when they came in for counseling. Jan began. "I must have more love and affection from you. And when I get upset, I must have more understanding instead of you saying, 'Never mind, it was nothing.' And once a month I must have you take me out, just you and me, away from the kids."

Dan told Jan his needs. "I must be able to go sailing for a few days each year and be able to do it without being nagged, without feeling bad before I go, and having it destroyed for me. I must have more understanding from you. I have to calm down and start meeting my responsibilities to you and the kids."

Brenda and Chris share willingness to help

Finally, partners share what they are each willing to do or give to make their relationship work. Chris had been pressuring Brenda for months to stop the divorce action, but she refused. The divorce weighed very heavily on his mind. "I'm willing to do something about my drinking. I'll give it up completely if necessary. I'm willing to give of myself and do whatever I can do to make us happy. I still have a lot of responsibility at work. I still won't be able to take off every time you want me to."

Brenda told Chris, "I'm willing to go to work to help us financially. It may cost a lot for sitters, but I'd be willing to do it. I'm willing to work on our marriage and work on communication to make it strong, so we can stay together forever and ever. It was difficult talking to you before. I felt that you were overpowering. I felt tongue-whipped. Now it's easier. I still love you. I'm willing to give it a try." Brenda told Chris she would set the divorce aside, providing he would agree to attend Alcoholics Anonymous for his drinking problem.

One couple experiencing the entire process

Donna and Bill came in for marriage counseling. They were plagued with serious problems. Their 13-year marriage was a second for each of them. Bill had a 20-year-old son, Andy, from his first marriage, and together Donna and Bill had a 10-year-old daughter, Jennifer. Donna was working part-time, and Bill was working full-time in his own business. During their sixth year together, Andy, then 13 years old, came to live with them. Donna perceived this event as the beginning of their marital problems. This couple exemplify the insidious way that ingrained resentments can undermine a couple's closeness, love, and trust. Because this was their first counseling session with me, I asked them each to describe how they perceived their relationship. Donna went first.

Donna:

"Andy came between us. He came first. This played into my abandonment issues. I'd scream. My needs came last. I was not being supported and I resented it. I was so angry. I was not allowed to get angry as a kid. I gradually became Stoic and took over the role of caretaker. I closed off and became cold to Bill, a ball of tension trying to protect myself. I couldn't share my feelings with Bill. It was a hard time. I became very depressed. To make matters worse, we were having serious financial pressures.

"Our life shifted when Andy came to live with us. Our daughter, Jennifer, and Andy didn't get along. I protected my child and tried to keep Andy happy. Andy and I had a good relationship while he lived with his mother, until he reached puberty. But as a teenager he was like a black hole. He was so needy that I started not wanting to give to him. I didn't trust men. I have always given more than I received.

"For the last year and a half, Andy has been living in his own apartment. Since he moved out, my relationship with Andy has improved. I think Andy was a scapegoat for our marital problems. I was never able to work past my resentments. Bill and I never discussed things regarding Andy coming to live with us. He expected me to accommodate his ex-wife. He didn't ask me what would work best for me."

After Donna had finished, Bill told how he perceived the situation.

Bill:

"Donna gave me mixed messages regarding Andy coming to live with us. After my divorce, I wanted Andy, but Andy was awarded to my ex-wife who moved out of state. I saw Andy only on vacations and holidays. After I married Donna, Donna pressured me to go to court for custody of Andy, but at that time I felt it was in no one's best interest. I believed that eventually when Andy was in his teens he would come to live with me.

"Donna said I didn't consider her as to when Andy would come to live with us. I never heard that before. I thought it was understood he would come that year. It never dawned on me she wanted to wait longer. Once Andy came out, Donna and Andy competed for my time. I think Donna would get even with me by attacking Andy. It was hard for me. I was angry that they couldn't see I loved both of them. It was difficult. I tolerated it and hoped it would go away.

"When Andy was in high school, Donna pushed to get Andy into a special school and then complained about transporting him there. I wouldn't have pursued it. It was a difficult time. We fought a lot and saw several counselors, but we always loved each other. I made a total commitment to her forever, but I found out she didn't feel that way.

"Donna feels she's the one who accommodates all the time. I do, too! I do what I can, and she feels what I do doesn't matter. Now we are trying to work on some issues and trying to give each other space to express ourselves without getting into childish responses. We're beginning to talk better, more open and honest."

Following these preliminaries, I described the Face-to-Face Communication Process and asked them to turn their chairs toward each other. Donna volunteered to begin first. I instructed her to begin the process by using the words "I resent" or "I resented," and to then state her resentments. I also asked Bill to listen until she finished without interrupting her. Donna shed many tears as she faced Bill and shared her resentments. Afterward, Bill shared his own resentments. In the beginning, he had a slight smile on his face, but toward the end, he, too, shed tears.

Part I: Donna and Bill share their resentments

Donna:

"Okay. I resented having to accommodate Andy when he came out and I had to quit my job to take care of him. I just didn't feel like you participated. I resent that you get time off at the end of your day because I never get time off. I may not be going out and working a job, but I sometimes think that might be easier. But you come home and have a drink while I'm finishing the laundry, helping with home-work, fixing dinner, and cleaning up. Then it's the bedtime routines and you're sitting in there that whole time. I don't want to be in charge of everything. I want to be your lover. I need your help. I want to work together. I resent that I was the one providing Andy's needs. I was the one who was listening and available. I resent that I was always the me-diator between you and Andy. I just get tired of always be-ing the harmonizer.

"I know a lot of times I just couldn't take it. It was be-cause I was always accommodating his needs no matter what time of day it was or what he did. It seemed like you were always there for him, not for me. That's why I always had those crises. I was just trying to get your attention. That's what I had to do as a child, and I know there are other options now. You were always defending Andy and now you're doing the same thing with Jennifer. I'm always the bad guy. It's always my fault. I have a right to be re-spected. You know Jennifer's the one who needs to have some boundaries. We need to be a team. I resent the fact that I have become defensive and hardened over the years. I feel like my voice is never heard.

"I know that you feel you're available to me now and we do talk more now, but for many years I had to deal with your crap and Andy's, and this brought in a lot of negativ-ity. When your last business failed, I was living in fear, afraid they'd take away our home, our car, and our furni-ture. We didn't even have money for Christmas gifts for Andy and Jennifer that year. It was a major trauma for them and for me. That's something from the past, a mem-ory obviously I needed to talk about because it happened.

"I resent having to live in this city all this time, in a place that I hate, to give you time to get your business together. Living in a city where you were raised, and all your friends and family live, and the people you always knew, and I don't have the freedom to be with my family.

Our holidays are spent with your family. It's hard for me and I do blame you for that because I wouldn't have stayed in California if it weren't for you.

"I resent taking care of you and you don't even take care of your own stuff. When Jennifer and I were sick and I made chicken noodle soup, you came home and ate it. I mean, come on. Take care of yourself! I just feel what I give and do for the family is not appreciated. I don't feel you know what it takes to get the family together and to do the meals and to create a homey atmosphere.

"I need to know that you love me for that and see me as a really big part of our life together. I feel I have accommodated a lot in the last 13 years. I need to know that we're making choices together. The part I resent is having to do the crap work. You know, it's fun to have a career and a job. You go out there and you get your strokes, and you come home and your closet is color coordinated with all of your shirts, and the kids are cared for, and you have a meal that's specifically designed and prepared for *you*, and then you get to go and have a drink and sit down and do nothing. I know you feel I get to spend time with my child and be a mother, and yes, that is true. But it's not true that I got to do it worry-free and supported."

Bill had listened attentively. Now he shared his resentments.

Bill:

"I resent your making an issue over one cup of soup that I had. Half a pot was thrown away two days later. I resent your interfering when I'm trying to mediate my relationship with my kids. I resent that you complain about housework. Not much housework is done. I resent the fact that you don't have a housekeeper. You've had two or three and nobody can clean well enough, so you let them go. I resent that you won't hire someone to do that stuff. I keep telling you to do it, and you refuse to do it. I resent that you don't hear my appreciation for all you do."

Bill paused, then said, "I don't have a lot of resentments."

I encouraged him to give himself a little more time, because this was his chance to bring up all his resentments. After a few moments, Bill continued.

"I resent your complaining about taking care of my car when yours is a total disaster. I resent your saying we don't make joint decisions. You make decisions that I wouldn't have made, like sending Andy to private school. Then you complain about having to drive him to school!"

Tears came to Bill's eyes. He reached for a tissue and held it to his eyes for a few moments, then he continued. "I understand where it's coming from but I'm...over-mothered when you step in while I'm disciplining Andy or Jennifer. That really neuters my relationship with them. I wish my mother would have stepped out of the relationship between me and my father." Bill cried openly. "When I'm telling my kids something, don't mix in. If you have something to tell me, take me aside. Don't start attacking me in front of the kids.

"I resent that you don't recognize the things that I do for the family and that I'm an equal participant. I resent you don't appreciate how many times you have gone back to visit your family. And that you don't hear all the times I've expressed my appreciation to you for all you do, like last year when you grew all those fresh vegetables!"

After Bill finished sharing his resentments, Donna added a few more of hers.

Donna:

"I resent the way you talk about how I like to control things. If we have debts we can't pay off, why incur a greater debt by hiring a housekeeper? Two years down the line, we may not be able to pay it off. I don't even know what our monthly income is. I resent being kept in the dark. I resent being expected to be Andy's birth mother. I resent that he was a junk-food junkie and overloaded with media when he came to us and that's all he knew. I cared more about what that child ate in a meal than his mother even cared about anything."

Bill:

"Yeah, you did."

Donna: (crying)

"It was expected. This is my nature. I am a caregiver, and I love children, and I loved Andy, and I still do love Andy. But I want someone to love me that way. I wish there was someone in my life that I knew could support me the way I supported him. It's not your fault. I'm not saying that it is. I resent that you brought so much pain into our relationship. There was so much to deal with. What I resent is that it was expected of me. Do you know I played that role at the expense of nurturing my own self? I just didn't feel appreciated. After Andy came to live with us, 'There's Donna the Witch', and I resent always being pictured that way when I've given my heart and soul, too."

Bill:

"I resent that you resent me for something I had nothing to do with. I resent the fact that you wanted to get Andy to come, and you gave him all this love and attention, and did this and that and the other thing. I didn't force you to or tell you to do it. You did it and now you resent me because you did it. I don't understand that. I resent that you can't allow me to be a parent, that you have to interfere."

Donna:

"We do need a mutual understanding. There's a better way to parent than the way your father and mother parented you. I resent the fact that I'm always the one being asked to change. I have changed a lot. It was that way in my first marriage. I was the only one who ever changed.

"When you and I were first married, I was doing your billing, and raising Jennifer, taking care of your car, and shopping and you weren't even working full-time. I know you have changed, but I really resented that. That picture came to my mind of me mowing the lawn with Jennifer in her little backpack on my back and the neighbor woman saying 'Donna, you're going to make us all look bad. Stop doing your own lawn.' That needed to come out, okay?"

Part II: Donna and Bill share their concerns

After sharing resentments for hours, Donna's and Bill's moods lightened up considerably. Both smiled and laughed as they shared their concerns.

Bill: (laughing)

"I'm concerned about getting my Mercedes taken care of."

Donna: (laughing)

"You are? (becoming serious) I'm a little concerned about growing faster than you. I'm hoping we will be able to be more free with each other. I'm concerned that we're spending too much time away from each other. When we have a disagreement, we stay apart for a while. Now, I don't know that we need to really be apart. Instead of you watching the news, you could come in and talk to me."

Bill laughed.

Donna:

"I still have a concern about your new business. I'm afraid to say this because I don't want to undermine your confidence. I have total confidence in what you're doing, but I do have that concern."

Bill:

"I think Jennifer's education is my concern. And our ability to mutually understand and find a way to motivate her. (pausing) That's all of my concerns."

Part III: Donna and Bill share their regrets

Bill:

"I regret, first of all, that I didn't inform you about my financial status when we got married. I regret that we haven't been able to work together more closely in terms of confidence. I regret that I wasn't more forceful with some of my ideas about Andy, and I regret procrastinating on so many things." Bill paused and nodded to Donna to proceed.

Donna:

"I regret Andy not being able to come to live with us from the beginning, because by the time he got here, he had so many problems. I regret we didn't get help when Andy did come to live with us full-time. We really needed some skills then that we didn't have. I regret those years that I went into my shell and was depressed. Now, fortunately, Andy wants to participate in the family.

"I regret how apart and alone I have felt. I regret not having another child."

Bill: (in tears)

"I regret I wasn't able to help you. (crying) There wasn't the trust before and I wasn't able to see. (After recovering his composure, he laughed.) I regret not taking out the bougainvillea clippings last night."

Donna: (in tears)

"I regret that Jennifer had to hear us fighting all those years and that Andy was robbed of the family we could have been for him. I regret that my family is so far away.

"I regret my years in a shell. (closing her eyes) I regret the struggle between Andy and me trying to have our needs met. (then smiling) I think I'm pretty well done."

After completing the first half of the Face-to-Face Communication Process, Donna commented, "It was like lancing the boil today, letting it all come out. This process is very powerful."

Donna and Bill returned one week later to complete the second half of the process. When asked how they felt during the interim week, Donna replied, "That process shifted our trust level. I feel so much more united, understood, and happy. Our relationship is lighter and more fun now."

Bill agreed and added, "There is a lighter feeling. Donna and I are more open with each other."

Part IV: Bill and Donna share what they want

During this session Donna and Bill completed the first part of the process by sharing what they each wanted. Bill went first.

Bill:

"Okay, I want Andy to do well and find his way. I want to be financially independent. I want to see you without concern about money. I want to be able to travel.

I want to figure out what to do with Jennifer's schooling. I want a different house, maybe in North Carolina or Arizona or northern New Mexico. I want to lose weight. I want to work together on helping Jennifer grow up. I want to see us continue to support each other, and be free and open with each other."

Donna:

"I want to play together more. I want to have fun together. I want to build a life together, and be grandparents together, and have a lot of fun doing it. I definitely want to empower Andy to find his way. I want him to be successful in his own mind. I want financial freedom so we don't have to be restricted to what area we live in. I want a house with space around it in a climate that has four seasons. It would be lovely to have running water on our property. We could go out and sit in the hammock and have our morning coffee and eat our meals outside.

"I would really like to read books together. We used to read to each other a lot. I just feel like sharing a book. I'd like to continue working on greater passion in our physical relationship. I want a weekend where we can be alone together, the two of us, maybe every four to six weeks. Now that would be nice and nurturing.

"I want to get our house in order, like a family trust. It would really feel good. I want someone to do the housekeeping for me and I would like to take some cooking classes. I want a home that's great for entertaining. I would really like to have friends over more often.

"I want to put Jennifer into an educational environment that engages her and really encourages her self-reliance. I want Andy to be a part of our life.

"If we're going to live in a city, I really want to be able to get out of town, even just to go camping locally. That's really nurturing to my soul. That's why it's so important.

"I'd like not having to drive Jennifer to school. That's a big one. I just like having my mornings free. I can't say career-wise what I want, but I feel that it's going to be in some kind of art. I guess what I'm asking for is the financial support and the time to invest in learning new skills.

"I would like to continue getting into shape so that I could go backpacking. I'd love to do that with you. I would like to find a church that we as a family could have as a community, especially before Jennifer becomes a teenager. That's something that we really don't have. Oh, I would like to have as many cats as I want."

Bill: (laughing)

"I could do without the cats. I do want vacations. I want to go to Alaska, Tahiti, the Caribbean, and to Egypt. I'd like to do a couple of those anyway. I want you to have the freedom to go see your family and do whatever you need to do. I want to take a trip alone together. We could fly Jennifer to see your folks."

Part V: Donna and Bill share what they each need

Donna:

"Well, I must have the freedom to be me, to continue learning new things and growing spiritually. I need to get out of the city more. I need to not live in the city. I don't know how that's going to happen right now, but I need to know that there's a time when I'm not going to have to live here. That's probably going to be when Jennifer's in high school.

"Something I didn't say is that we really need to continue growing in our communication skills as a family. I don't think we have it together. We love each other, and we're really fortunate in that, and we have a lot of great things working for us. But it would be fun to be able to work together as a family, and play together, too. I think we're finding our way. I need us to become more clear about our parenting skills with Jennifer. I need to understand what you're doing, what's okay and what's not, and consequences for things that aren't okay. Soon she's going to be a teenager.

"I want to start taking the emotion out and being clear about our disagreements instead of, 'You were to do this' and 'I was to do this.' To be able to stop the drama and just be responsible for our own actions. I need to do that. We need to have an agreement, because otherwise we fall back into a really ugly cycle. I need to stop that.

"I need time at home alone in our house to get our home in order. I was happy you weren't home last night. I got so much done without interruption. I need at least one full day at home alone. I need to get in a carpool because I really hate that drive to school.

"I need respect and appreciation for what I do and personal respect for who I am. I need you to not be demeaning to me when you talk to me. We need to clarify for our family what's an okay way for us to express anger. It's going to happen. We're not perfect. (pausing) I think I'm done, really. Those are my needs."

Bill:

"I need to have you support me as a father to Jennifer and Andy. I need to get my stuff out of the house and get an office. I really need to play golf at least once a week. I need to continue working out. I need to lose weight. I also need more time away from the city, and we can do that. We can make that happen time-wise even if we have to primarily live here. We can still get more time away.

"I need you to hear my affirmation of you as a person and what you do around the house. I need you to recognize that even though we may be doing different things, we're still moving together, that we're on the same journey, that we have the same goals, really. I need you to let me love you like I need to. I need you to receive my love. I need you to open up and allow me to love you without being afraid. I need you to support me with Jennifer and allow me to be a father without interrupting, regardless of whether you think I'm right or wrong. We can talk about it between the two of us, but not in front of Jennifer.

"I need you to continue to believe in my new business. I need you to get a housekeeper. If I say something's okay, you can trust me. I need to show you that I support you as a person. That's what I need from you."

Donna:

"You know, Bill, I do need you to lose weight. I need to have a better intellectual grip on how you are parenting Jennifer. That would help me to let go. If I knew there was actually a formula, not just doing it the way we were raised—which was dominating and fear tactics. That's why I step in, because it feels so much like what I had when I was growing up, that I can't tolerate it anymore. I need to hear from you about how you are parenting and how you are providing guidance."

Bill:

"If we disagree, I need you not to do it in front of her."

Part VI: Donna and Bill share their willingness to help

Donna:

"I'm willing to be more open with you. I will try. I'm willing to work on our parenting skills regarding Jennifer. It definitely needs work.

(laughing) "You can take me away for a week whenever you want. (pausing) I'm willing to continue supporting your new business. I don't think I'm doing anything to help except for believing in you right now and praying for you. But I do believe."

Bill:

"Well, I'm willing to continue losing weight. I'm willing to work together with Jennifer on trying to motivate her and get her behavior under control. I'm willing to open up with the finances and let you know where everything is. I'm willing to continue trying to get through your thick skull that you are appreciated and loved on a daily basis. I'm willing to get out of town more and use the time-share a lot more. I'm willing to support your taking different classes, and I'm willing to read together as we used to. I'm willing to support you in getting a housekeeper. I'm willing to spend more one-on-one time together."

Donna:

"I think I hear the appreciation, but what's hard is that in the heat of anger when you have all this energy behind you, you become very critical. So it's like the appreciation is this little trickle, but then the criticism is like this lion. It's like in the face of the lion, the mouse runs away."

As this session and the process came to an end, Donna and Bill both agreed to return for another counseling session to work on parenting and dealing with their anger, because these were the two issues they fought about most. This Face-to-Face Communication Process is not a panacea, but its structure allows couples to express themselves on a deep level and be heard. This can lead to a closer relationship. I have observed it over and over again, couples who were ready to separate deciding to make a new beginning. And even though couples may still split up, sometimes this communication work leads to a smoother separation instead, and more willingness to cooperate afterward regarding children who may be involved.

Putting it in writing

If desired, couples can write out all six parts of the Face-to-Face Communication Process, taking as much time as they wish, and then share it with each other afterward. If you choose to try this method, you should each use a separate page or pages for each part of the process: 1) resentments, 2) regrets, 3) concerns, 4) wants, 5) needs, and 6) what you are willing to do or give to make your relationship work. *A word of caution:* Do not argue about what your partner says. This defeats the whole purpose.

I remember one very angry woman who wrote 18 pages of resentments. Her husband said he didn't realize she had so many resentments. By the time she had finished, she said, "I got a lot off my chest, and I don't feel so tense and angry anymore."

Even when couples have done the process in writing, I suggest they do all six parts verbally afterward, facing each other without notes.

When verbal communication is not possible

Verbal communication is not always possible. When it is not, there are alternative ways to express your feelings. When you sense it best not to verbally reveal intense feelings to your partner, you can pour out your resentments in other ways, so you can get them out of your system. One method is to write a letter, that you may or may not let your partner read. The other is to put your resentments on tape. By the time you have written or taped your resentments, you should feel much calmer and more controlled. Then you might be able to communicate these feelings verbally to your partner in a calmer, more constructive manner that will leave you and your partner feeling good about each other.

Writing your resentments. The act of writing your feelings can be very therapeutic and releasing, especially if verbal communication is extremely difficult for you, or if your partner has a problem listening or can't control his or her temper. Writing also gives you the chance to think your communication through very carefully, so that you can express yourself completely. Write a letter to your partner that you will not let him or her see. Write down all of your resentments using any format you like. (You don't have to use "I" messages in this letter.) Express your pain and anguish. Tell it all and imagine yourself saying it to your partner as you write. Then tear up your letter in a thousand pieces and throw it away along with the resentments you expressed in the letter.

If you decide you want to write a letter that your partner will read, I suggest you use the "I" message format to avoid putting your partner on the defensive. Express your feelings in terms of your own experience. For example: "I resent the way you put me down in front of the children and other people." The "I" message format is likely to bring about the best results in terms of your relationship with your partner. Putting it in writing and sending or leaving the letter for your partner to read (when you are not there), gives your partner the chance to read and reread your feelings. After the first reading, your partner may feel defensive, but become more receptive to your message after the second or third reading.

Taping your resentments. Putting your resentments on tape, then listening to the tape, and erasing the tape is another very simple yet therapeutic technique for dealing with feelings that cannot be communicated to your partner directly. Taping resentments can be especially helpful if you feel uncontrollable rage that could get out of hand or jeopardize your relationship with your partner.

To use this taping method, I suggest you set aside one hour when you are out of earshot and won't be disturbed. You can use your car for this purpose if you have no other completely private space available. Speak into the tape recorder as if you were speaking directly to the person with whom you wish to communicate. You can yell and scream if you like and say exactly what you think and feel, including all of your resentments. Afterward, rewind the tape, listen to it once or twice, then erase or destroy it along with the resentments you expressed.

The importance of clearing away resentments cannot be overemphasized. First, imagine a stream jammed with logs and debris so that the water can barely flow. Only when the debris is removed or released can that stream flow freely again. Relationships are like streams. To be free-flowing and alive, they cannot be dammed up with anger, hurt, and frustration. Only when these resentments are cleared away can the love and intimacy flow freely.

CHAPTER 3

Expressing Anger Maturely

To feel angry is natural. How we express anger makes the difference between getting what we need and getting into trouble. Throughout my years of counseling, many couples have described negative outcomes that result when anger gets out of control. A young woman, Cathy, described being choked by her husband while their frightened children looked on. Afterward, Cathy said she was unable to love or trust her husband again. Doug, married for more than 25 years, told me he was divorcing his wife because he couldn't stand her verbally abusive tirades anymore.

Anger is the emotion that wells up inside of us when we feel hurt, frustrated, threatened, afraid, humiliated, or discounted. Because anger is a natural defense mechanism designed to protect us from pain and abuse, it is not wise to deny feeling angry.

Instead, it is beneficial to feel and acknowledge angry feelings when they do occur. But remember, angry feelings are not the problem; out of control anger can lead to big problems.

It is natural for us to want what we want when we want it. As infants we screamed when we didn't get our way immediately. Little children kick and scream and throw tantrums when they are angry, and may even try to hit those who won't give them their way. For some individuals, this tantrum-throwing behavior continues into adulthood. Impatience in adulthood is a continuation of our desire to have our needs met immediately. Part of growing up has to do with being able to delay gratification, and not act out all of our feelings. When we are hurt or frustrated, we might feel like punching someone or breaking something, but we can put the brakes on our behavior, much in the same way we put our foot on the brake to stop our car. If we were to let our car run away with us, we would surely crash. Likewise, when we allow feelings to run us or run away with us, we are not in charge. Then we can cause damage to ourselves and our loved ones. Unbridled angry, bitter arguments and fights tend to breed tension and hostility, not love.

Some individuals find it easier to tolerate frustration and control impulses than others. This is in part due to individual, constitutional, and temperamental differences, as well as how individuals were raised. None of us can help how we feel, but *we can help what we do*. When a situation becomes "too hot to handle," partners should separate for an hour or so to let things calm down, and then later discuss what caused the upset. It can be extremely dangerous to insist that a problem be discussed when one partner is ready to explode.

To emphasize this point, following is a description of a terrible fight that need never have happened: It started out as a discussion that escalated into an argument. Paul became extremely upset and wanted to leave the house to calm down, but Suzanne wouldn't let him leave. She grabbed his keys and held onto him. Paul pushed her away and ran to his car. Suzanne ran outside, opened the car door, and tried to pull him out. Paul managed to close the door again and lock it. However, Suzanne laid on the car so he couldn't drive away. Paul then got out of the car and beat her up. Neighbors called the police, and Suzanne was taken to the hospital. This violence and near tragedy could have been prevented. For couples such as Paul and Suzanne, therapy is essential. Without professional help, relationships and lives can be lost.

As adults, it is up to each of us to break out of immature patterns of expressing anger, whether it be acting out angry impulses or holding anger inside and not expressing it at all. We are each responsible for our own behavior, and if motivated, we can develop new patterns for expressing anger that can serve us well and help us feel proud, not ashamed.

The three processes presented here each have a special place and purpose in supporting a positive shift and growth toward a mature way of expressing anger:

1. *The Process for Evaluating Old Patterns for Expressing Anger* is designed to assist you in reviewing incidents throughout your life when you felt most angry and in evaluating your old patterns. This process should be done only once.

2. *The Process for Establishing New Patterns for Expressing Anger* is designed to assist you in developing new, mature patterns for expressing anger. This process should be repeated often until new patterns are firmly established.

3. *The Process for Screaming Away Anger* affords physical and emotional relief at times of intense distress. This process can be repeated as often as needed.

Evaluating Old Patterns for Expressing Anger

As we grow from infancy to adulthood, we each develop certain patterns for expressing anger. Some patterns are constructive and serve us, while others are destructive. When patterns are destructive, we usually pay a very high price by hurting ourselves and our loved ones. This process can assist you in evaluating old patterns of expressing anger throughout your life and give you insight, both into what you do and what you may want to change.

For best results, this process should be done by both partners together, first by one partner leading the other through it, and then vice versa; or both partners being led through the process, one at a time, by a therapist (again, both partners are present). Following is an example of the latter as I led both Donna and Bill through this process.

Donna is led through the process

Donna and Bill were both raised by parents who did not allow anger to be expressed. During their 13-year marriage, the way they each expressed their anger became a major problem for them as a couple. During their last counseling session with me, they had shared the Face-to-Face Communication Process (see Chapter 2) and afterward agreed to return again to work on their anger. First, I led Donna through the Process for Evaluating Old Patterns of Expressing Anger while Bill listened. Then, I led Bill through it while Donna listened.

To begin the process, I asked Donna to remember a time as a child when she felt the most angry. Donna sat quietly and closed her eyes. She paused awhile and then replied, "I wasn't allowed to express my anger as a child. So it came out in different ways. I remember fighting with my sister a lot. Julie and I would wrestle, hold each other down on the bed, and pull each other's hair."

I asked Donna if she considered her behavior appropriate, considering her age and circumstances. Donna's reply was, "No, no, not at all." When I queried if she thought the way she handled it caused her to feel better or worse, about herself afterward, Donna replied, "Probably worse because I usually had to pay the price with my parents. I usually got the belt from my father."

"So what did your response cost you?" I asked. Donna replied, "Pain, humiliation, slavery. It was total embarrassment. Like a pressure cooker, that was the only outlet I had with my sister."

I asked Donna, "If you had the chance to do it over again, what would you do differently?"

Donna thought for a moment, then replied, "I'd try to resolve it together. I'd realize that these are stupid little things, not worth giving up your love for a person over. I'd be more objective about what's going on and realize how meaningless it really is."

A particular incident came to Donna's mind. When she was in the tenth grade, her father had whipped her. When I asked her if she felt angry with her father, Donna replied, "I didn't feel anger. No, because in the church I was taught from the time I was little that this is the way it's supposed to be, that your parents love you and the Bible teaches: 'Spare the Rod and Spoil the Child.' So, to me, you just had to endure. I couldn't be angry at my father; that's what God had told him to do. What was I going to do, be angry at God? So I was just ashamed and I was hurt, and it hurt. I didn't think about lashing back in any way. If I did, he might have hit me with the belt in my face. That might even have happened to me at one time."

I asked Donna if she would review that incident in her mind again and attach a different ending to this story. "The reason my father stepped in was because we were given boundaries as children with what was okay with our anger and when we crossed those boundaries, then he stepped in. We were punished for not adhering to the boundaries. A different ending might be that Dad would have taken us to the kitchen table, sat us down with a glass of lemonade and said, 'Okay, girls, look at each other. Look at the face of your sister. Is this really what you want to do to her body?' He could have taught us how to deal with our anger and given us some skills. I don't think that when I was still at home I could think of anger. Everything was always manipulated to make sure that it didn't come out."

Donna then explained that things changed when she was 18, after there was a man in her life who abused her. "The incident that made me really angry was on my birthday. I remember I was in the back of a van. It was safe for me to get angry because my boyfriend was driving and there were several seats between us. I felt really enraged. That was the first time I ever remember just losing control."

I encouraged Donna to review the entire incident in her mind. Donna reminisced, "He hadn't planned anything for my birthday. I was screaming, pounding on the seat, and hurting my body from screaming. I have become so controlling because I don't want things like this to happen. I have to protect myself from that ever happening."

I asked Donna if, looking back at that event, she felt she had handled her anger in an appropriate, constructive way, considering her age and circumstance.

Immediately Donna said, "No. When I went through that rage I felt just like a baby. It was a very euphoric, weird feeling. Afterward, I just lay down, got in a sleeping bag in the back of the van, and went to sleep. Maybe that was like a lifetime catharsis of some sort because I didn't have to carry the weight anymore. My body was totally drained."

I asked Donna if her angry outburst caused problems for her afterward.

"Well, sure. I had to rebuild that relationship. It actually created fear in me because it made me wonder if I could control myself. It was scary for me, and Max, my boyfriend, probably never recovered from that. I think he made a commitment that he would always do something for my birthday. Two years later when I turned 21, we were still together and I got a chocolate ice cream cone. That was really exciting."

I encouraged Donna to visualize a different ending for that incident in the van, but Donna explained why she could not: "If I try to resolve it or handle too much, I really don't know how to do that. I still don't."

Moving on in this process, next I asked Donna to recall an incident that happened in her 20s. Donna described the following: "It was the same man, Max, and he started it. I was trying to make dinner and he was getting angry and violent. I tried to get out of the apartment. I had to leave when he got like that. But he wouldn't let me leave, so I went in the bedroom and I didn't get the door closed and locked in time. He opened it up and he hit me in the eye. That was the angriest I ever was. I was trapped in the corner screaming like an animal basically. I just had to give up because, in the face of his anger, I knew there was no way out."

I asked, "Looking back, would you evaluate your response as appropriate and constructive considering your age and circumstances?"

"I was such a victim," Donna replied. "No, it wasn't appropriate. I mean in ongoing abusive relationships, you lose a sense of reality. People don't live this way. It's very sick. I was near suicidal a couple of times."

To my question, "What other way could you have handled this situation?" she replied, "I could have left him a lot sooner than I did and taken care of myself again."

Finally, moving toward the present, I asked Donna if she could recall a recent event that brought up a lot of anger in her. At first Donna couldn't recall a recent incident, but after a few moments, she described an incident that happened three years earlier: "We were having an argument about something, probably about our daughter, Jennifer. So, it's escalating. I went into the hall and Bill slapped me to get me out of my rage, I guess. It really hurt. After he slapped me, my neck was killing me. Bill said, 'Oh, I didn't even touch you.' He totally demeans you for having any kind of feeling at all. Jennifer was right there in her room. Bill was screaming, and I was just screaming back at Bill. I might have kicked him, I don't know. I remember I shut the door, got my pillow and screamed into my pillow until I was hoarse. I swore to myself this would never happen again. I'd like to have a healthy family. I'd like to get to that point where we're not treating each other that way and be able to heal from that. We're both willing to learn whatever skills it takes to support one another to be healthy and happy together, not to be outraged and angry."

Once again I asked Donna, "Would you review the last incident again and visualize yourself attaching a different ending to this story?"

Donna said, "I think I'd say, 'Bill, let's take time out and tomorrow at five o'clock, let's talk about this, because we can't deal with it now.' What I envision or imagine is regularly working on communication skills and resolving issues, then going forward as partners instead of having our own worlds and getting professional help when we need it."

Bill is led through the process

I asked Bill to close his eyes and recall a time as a child when he was the most angry. Bill's response was, "I don't remember specific incidents of anger as a child. Donna and I were raised pretty much the same way. I wasn't allowed to display anger. I used to feel frustrated, but not angry. Actually, my whole childhood I used to get frustrated with my grandmother until she died. She was always a major pain in the butt. It wasn't anger, but I was always frustrated because everything revolved around her and she was so controlling. I guess I was around 2 years old or so. I was trained that whenever we came home I would open the door and say, 'ladies first.' So for my entire life when she was around, I could never walk through a door without having to do that, and it got a little old after a while. She used to come over to the house for dinner on Sundays and she and my dad used to argue quite a bit. She was a snob and she was always talking about cleaning this and cleaning that and how clean she was. It was always frustrating because my mother was totally controlled by my grandmother, and they used to really put my dad down."

I asked Bill how he handled his frustration at that time and Bill replied, "I had to stuff it, but I dealt with it by trying not to be there. I never played at home unless I had to. I knew two or three other families who treated me like they were my own family, and when I was in junior high and high school, I spent as much time as I could there for dinners and sleep-overs, more than I was at home. I'd play a lot of sports and physical stuff. I wasn't allowed to really be angry."

I asked Bill, "What other way could you have handled your frustration? If you had the chance to do it over again, would you do it differently?"

Bill replied, "I was always trying to be this perfect little boy for her, because I was an extension of them. I think I'd have been more of my own person, but that was the way children were raised, not to be heard. So I don't know if I could have done it differently at that time."

Bill was unable to recall any incidents in his early or late teens. However, when I asked him to recall incidents in his 20s, he described the following: "I recall getting mad for the first time when I was married to my first wife. I was 24 or 25 then. She started pestering me. My first fight with her was over the fact that I wouldn't fight with her. She just started arguing with me about the fact that I never fought. I didn't know what I was supposed to fight about, so she started saying things that would get me upset. I didn't respond, so she locked herself in the bathroom and started calling me names. I said that this is stupid; there's nothing to fight about. I don't remember if I left or just disengaged or what, but for the first time, I was angry because I couldn't figure out why somebody would be angry about my not being angry."

I asked Bill to evaluate if, looking back at that event and his response, he had handled this anger in an appropriate and constructive way considering his age and circumstances." Bill's response was, " I probably should have divorced her sooner."

Next, I encouraged Bill to recall a recent incident when he felt very angry. Bill then described the same incident that Donna had referred to from his own perspective: "Donna was upset. I don't recall what it was about exactly, but I was responding to her saying what I wasn't doing that she felt I should or shouldn't have done. I was on the defensive for who I was or what I had or hadn't done, and she just kept going on and on and screaming and yelling, and I couldn't say anything.

Donna won't let you. She just screams louder. So in our mis-communications, I'm the one who can't communicate and I'm always the one who can't talk. Anyway, she just kept going on and on, and I just responded to my anger. I don't know what happened first but I did slap her, trying to get her attention. I wasn't hitting her like Max did, but afterward, I said I didn't even hit her, referring to the fact that I wasn't hitting her out of anger as much as I was trying to get her to realize that she was out of control. I might have also hit her in the leg once and I remember being kicked and scratched and bitten and hit by her. Once I broke the bathroom door down. But all those things were in response to having no control over the situation and it was basically the frustration of what I had swallowed and put up with from my childhood."

When I asked Bill if he felt his behavior was appropriate, and how he felt afterward, he replied, "It wasn't Donna's fault. It was my fault and I didn't know how to handle it, because I had never been allowed to have anger and I didn't know how to express it."

I encouraged Bill to review this incident again, choosing a response that he believed more desirable. Bill reviewed the incident and stated, "I allowed myself to get sucked in by Donna's frustrations. I wanted Donna to accept me. If she accepted me for who I was, then I would perform and take care of her needs. Essentially that's the grandmother stuff I think, because I was always trying to be accepted. I always wanted to tell them, 'I'm okay. You guys are always telling me I need to do this, I need to do that, and I'm really okay.' I think that with Donna, I was trying to get her to accept me like my parents and grandmother didn't. I think now that's not something I need to do. I mean, there are things I need to do that are my responsibility. I need to take responsibility as far as the physical aspect. Three years ago we made an agreement and I've gotten angry since then, but I haven't responded physically. I really don't have that need to do it because it's my stuff, and when Donna gets under my skin, or when she used to get under my skin, it was really my issues with my parents and my grandmother. It was not about her."

I gave Bill and Donna my perspective: "I feel especially sad that both of you had to go through this. When children aren't allowed to acknowledge or express anger, it is bound to come up over and over again in relationships. A nurturing relationship is a safe place for healing to take place. Being able to experience and express anger is beneficial, but there must be limits to acting out behavior. I know of families that have holes in the walls from their kids fighting. I didn't allow that, but my children were allowed to express their anger. Once, my daughter, at 14, yelled, 'I hate you' to me because I wouldn't let her go away camping without adult supervision. An hour or so later, she came and hugged me. I had made no issue about her outburst. She had calmed down and gotten over it."

Instructions for Evaluating Old Patterns for Expressing Anger

Whenever possible, ask your partner to lead you through this process, because this experience can help expand communication and closeness. The time required for each person to complete the process is between one and two undisturbed hours.

Caution: If there have been any incidents of physical violence between you, I urge you to seek the assistance of a mental health professional to lead you through this process.

Step 1.   Sit quietly and close your eyes. Recall an incident when you were a young child when you were most angry. If there are two or more competing incidents, focus on one of them now. Proceed to Step 2 and end with Step 6. If there were competing incidents, afterward focus on each of them, one at a time, using Steps 2 through 6 for each incident.

Step 2. Review in your mind how the incident or event that caused you to feel angry took place: How old were you then? What were you angry about? With whom were you angry? What happened to cause your anger? Who was present during the incident? What were they doing or saying that caused you to be angry? What were you doing or saying?

Step 3. Visualize yourself going back to that time. You might experience some anger as you reflect on the incident or event.

Step 4. Recall how you responded to your anger: How did you express your anger at that time? What did you do? What did you say? How did you behave?

Step 5. Looking back at that incident and your response to your anger, do you think that you expressed your anger appropriately, considering your age and circumstances at that time? Did the way you express your anger cause you to feel better or worse about yourself afterward? Did it cause problems for you afterward? What did your response cost you?

Step 6. What other way could you have expressed your anger in that instance? If you had the chance to do it over again, what would you do differently? Review the same incident or event again in your mind and visualize yourself attaching a different ending to the story. Choose a response that you believe would have been more desirable than the one you chose at that time.

Step 7. Recall an incident that made you most angry in your early adolescent years. Return to Step 2 and end with Step 6. Afterward, proceed to Step 8.

Step 8. Next, recall an incident that made you most angry in your late adolescent years. Follow the instructions again beginning with Step 2 and ending with Step 6. Afterward, proceed to Step 9.

Step 9. Recall an incident or event that made you most angry when you were in your 20s. Follow Steps 2 through 6, then proceed to Step 10.

Step 10. Recall an incident that happened recently that made you very angry. Follow Steps 2 through 6. It is not unusual after recalling stressful incidents to remain in the mood of the incident for a brief period of time. Should this occur, allow yourself to experience your feelings fully, *but do not act out your anger.*

Leading oneself through the process

In case you have no one, or wish no one, to lead you through this process, you can lead yourself through it. Following is an example of how I led myself through one portion of this process to evaluate my own behavior patterns after an incident from my childhood. I begin with Step 1, because I am examining an incident from my childhood. I recall an incident that made me most angry when I was a child. I then proceed to Step 2 and review in my mind the entire incident that caused my anger.

When I was about 8, I was expecting my best girlfriend for lunch. I was very excited. My mother and I had gone to a lot of trouble fixing a special lunch for her, including a special dessert. I was so excited that I went outside to wait for her. Diane lived across the street and up the block. I saw her and another girl walking toward my house on the other side of the street. I yelled, "Diane, lunch is almost ready. Come on over." She yelled back, "I'm not coming to your house, I'm eating over at my friend's house." I can't even remember that girl's name, but I was devastated. I felt totally betrayed. In fact, I was so furious that I didn't speak to Diane for two years, and she had been my best girl-friend. I continued to hold a grudge for all that time. By the time I was ready to talk to her again, we were total strangers. We never were friends again after that incident.

During Step 3, I visualize myself as a child again, feeling very angry when this incident occurred. Then I proceed to Step 4. During Step 4, I recall how I responded and how I expressed my anger. I continued to feel hurt and refused to forgive her for rejecting me. I didn't express my hurt or anger to her at all. I kept it all inside and held onto that grudge for two years.

During Step 5, I evaluate my behavioral response during and after the incident and examine how my response made me feel and what my response cost me.

Looking back on this event, I think my response was very extreme and inappropriate. Holding a grudge for two years because a friend broke a luncheon date seems now like a gross overreaction on my part. At that time, it apparently was very important to me to be *first* with Diane. I was not willing to forgive her when she put another friend first. The way I chose to handle my anger at that time was damaging for me. First of all, it caused me to lose my best friend. Also, carrying a grudge for all that time took a lot of my own energy, which could have been used for more satisfying purposes. In short, my response to the incident with Diane cost me a lot and I probably hurt her, too. I heard from another girl that Diane couldn't understand why I wouldn't talk to her. At first, she had tried to make up, but I ignored her, and finally she gave up.

Lastly, I proceed to Step 6. I examine what other ways I could have expressed my anger toward Diane. Then I review this incident again and visualize myself attaching a more positive ending to this story.

Thinking now about other ways I could have expressed my anger, I think the best choice would have been to tell Diane how angry I felt because she broke her promise to have lunch with me. I could have refused to play with her for a few days, then made up. I also could have gone over to that other girl's house and asked them both to come for lunch. I could have invited someone else for lunch. Mainly, I should have told Diane how I was feeling rather than keeping it all inside. Looking back, it amazes me how long I kept my anger going.

As I recreate the event, I visualize myself yelling to Diane to come over for lunch, and her saying, "No, I'm going to play with another friend." I visualize myself walking across the street and confronting her about her promise and inviting both of them to come over. Then I visualize all of us going over to my house and having lunch together. This response would have averted a two-year bitterness, which caused me a lot of pain, and the friendship of my best friend.

After I reviewed this particular incident and the way I held a grudge for two years at such a young age, I realized that I had also held two other grudges for even longer periods of time. This realization was helpful and has been healing for me.

Establishing New Patterns for Expressing Anger

Awareness of one's behavior is a first step toward growth. There must also be great desire and motivation to change one's behavior. The process just presented was designed to assist you in reviewing past incidents throughout your life and to evaluate your behavior and response patterns. The process presented next will assist you in developing and establishing new patterns for expressing anger. This process requires approximately one-half hour of undisturbed time and should be done as soon as possible after each time you feel angry, until new response patterns are strongly entrenched.

Step 1.   Sit down and close your eyes.

Step 2.   Recall the *last* incident that occurred when you felt angry, or you had an argument or fight. Review the incident in your mind.

Step 3. Recall how you responded and behaved. What did you do or say? How did you act?

Step 4. Take a few extra minutes to examine the incident again.

Step 5. If that incident, argument, or fight were happening right now, think about how you would want to respond. What change would you want to make?

Step 6. Visualize the whole incident happening again, and this time imagine yourself responding in a way that you wish you had responded. Select a way of responding and behaving that helps you feel good about yourself afterward, and proud of the way you handled your anger.

Each time you feel angry or have an argument or fight, take the time afterward to do this process. Gradually you will begin to see yourself as a growing person who learns from your experiences. As you develop new patterns, you will feel better about yourself and your loved ones.

Process for Screaming
Away Anger

As infants and young children, we screamed whenever we were upset, hurt, or angry. Yet screaming is considered inappropriate and immature for adults. Adults who resort to yelling, screaming, or tantrums in public or even at home lose self-respect and the respect of loved ones, especially when they become verbally abusive or physically violent. However, screaming when we are alone can afford both physical and emotional release. Screaming to release anger and tension for therapeutic purposes has no negative side effects, because the screaming is done in private, and no one has to even know about it. The worst thing that can happen from screaming done by oneself in private is a bit of hoarseness the next day.

Screaming away anger is a very simple, therapeutic way of releasing tension and anger, especially when it is difficult, impossible, undesirable, or unwise to communicate directly with the person with whom we are angry. Screaming can give relief when we are very upset, and this release makes it easier to communicate our feelings afterward.

Instructions for Screaming Away Anger

Step 1. To begin this process, set aside 30 to 45 minutes when you will not be disturbed, and not be within hearing range of other people. You may wish to use your car for this purpose so you can yell and scream as loud as you wish.

Step 2. Imagine yourself there with the person who has caused you to be angry. Scream out your rage, pain, anger, and resentments, or whatever feelings accompany your anger. Give yourself permission to cry and sob. Continue screaming until you feel calm, relaxed, and tired out.

Step 3. Follow this process with a brief nap or quiet, relaxing walk.

10 helpful strategies for handling anger

1. *When you are angry, take a few minutes to calm down.* Identify what feeling is causing your anger. Anger wells up when we feel frustrated, threatened, afraid, humiliated, rejected,

hurt, or jealous. Sort out which one of these feelings lies beneath your anger. Ask yourself, "What am I really feeling in this situation? Am I feeling hurt, or frustrated, or threatened, or jealous, or rejected, or humiliated, or unloved?

2. *Once you have identified the feeling beneath your anger, tell your partner what you are feeling and what you want your partner to do about it.* Whatever your feeling is, say it without sarcasm, name calling or vindictiveness. Use an "I" message. For example, if you feel humiliated, you might say, "I feel so humiliated when you put me down in front of other people. I am furious with you. I don't want you to ever do this again." If you feel jealous, you might say, "I felt very jealous when you flirted with that woman. I want you to consider my feelings and never do that again when I'm around."

3. *Avoid making statements that can devastate your partner or destroy your relationship.* Statements such as, "I'm leaving you," or "I want a divorce," or "Get out," or "You're no good," can cause *irreparable* harm. One husband repeatedly told his wife to leave every time he got angry with her. One day she packed her bags and left. When he came home from work and discovered she was gone, he was devastated. Afterward, during a mediation session with both of them, his wife told me that she had heard it once too often, she felt unloved, and decided that the next time he told her to leave, she would. She was not willing to come back.

4. *Avoid making sarcastic remarks, insults, put-downs, or subtle digs.* If your partner has done or said something to anger or upset you, instead of coming back with sarcasm or insults, share these feelings with your partner. In this way, your partner can become more mindful of what upsets you.

5. *If necessary, take a cooling-off period.* When you feel you're losing control of your temper, take a break or a short walk by yourself to sort things out. Then, later when you calm down, discuss the situation that has upset you.

6. *Above all, avoid hitting, pushing, shaking, grabbing, striking, or physically abusing your partner in any way,* even if you feel like doing it. Domestic violence is a criminal offense. If you feel you can't control yourself, leave the scene. Love and fear cannot exist together at the same time. If your partner fears you, he or she can't really love you. When fear enters the scene, love usually turns to hate.

7. *Find constructive ways to vent your anger.* Physical exertion and sports make good outlets, as does screaming away your anger in private.

8. *After you have calmed down, examine what part you had in creating the incident that angered you.* Once you come to see that you have some part in what happens to you, you will begin to feel more in control of your life and less apt to blame others.

9. *Repeat the Process for Establishing New Patterns for Expressing Anger* each time you slip back into inappropriate, immature ways of expressing anger.

10. *Seek professional help* immediately if you are physically or verbally abusing your partner and continue in therapy until you are able to control your behavior.

CHAPTER 4

Reducing Tension and Anxiety

In your quest to improve your relationship, stress-reduction skills should be placed high on your list of relationship safeguards. A certain amount of stress can be expected from everyday life, but when stress levels rise above those we can comfortably cope with, we then experience stress as "distress." For our purposes here, I am defining stress as emotional, mental, or physical tension or strain, urgency, pressure, or adversity.

The amount of stress each person can handle varies greatly from individual to individual. Some people can handle high levels of stress in stride, while others seem to go to pieces over very little stress. For each of us, there is a delicate balance between the level of stress we experience at a given time and our own unique stress tolerance. Imagine a scale: On one side is an individual's stress level at a particular point in time; on the other side, place that same individual's stress tolerance. When stress levels exceed an individual's stress tolerance, symptoms are likely to develop. Symptoms can include muscle tightness, especially around the head, neck, shoulders, chest, back, and stomach; headaches; neck aches; backaches; stomach aches; indigestion; constipation; insomnia; fatigue; lack of energy; anxiety; irritability; temper tantrums; poor appetite or tendency to overeat; and feelings of frustration, anxiety, helplessness, hopelessness, despair, and depression.

Each individual's stress tolerance is determined predominately by genetic and constitutional differences, temperamental differences, and environmental factors. Other pertinent factors include the timing and cause of the stress; an individual's physical condition and fatigue level at the time of stress; whether stress is situational and of short duration, or chronic and of long duration; and the amount of stress an individual has been exposed to in the past.

For most people, the following events or conditions are experienced as stressful:

➤ Becoming overwhelmed, overworked, overburdened, or overscheduled.

➤ Being ill or having a loved one become ill.

➤ Death of a loved one.

➤ Divorce or divorce of a loved one.

➤ Problems in relating to a husband, wife, partner, parent, child, boss, co-worker, or friend.

➤ Having a baby.

➤ Financial hardship or indebtedness.

➤ Business reversal.

➤ Being overextended financially or being unemployed.

➤ Having too many commitments.

➤ Having burn-out, or too little rest, sleep, or recreation.

➤ Surgeries, injuries, or accidents.

➤ Dental work.

➤ Overly strenuous exercise, over-exertion, or over-training without being in shape for it.

➤ Exercising without stretching or preparing the body.

➤ Overeating, or eating wrong foods.

➤ Obesity or being underweight.

➤ Smoking, alcohol, drug abuse, or too much caffeine or stimulants.

➤ Environmental stress such as smog or noise pollution.

Even when we are able to cope, too much stress still takes its toll on us. Medical authorities tell us that between 50 and 80 percent of all illness is stress-related. In addition to this astounding impact of stress on our health, the negative impact on our relationships is probably comparable, making stress-reduction skills essential.

On the brighter side, we can do much to reduce stress and the harm it can cause:

1. By learning to relax at will.

2. By making positive lifestyle changes and learning how to defuse tension in our relationships.

3. By exchanging negative attitudes and behavior patterns that cause stress for more life-affirming ones.

With a simple, dynamic repertoire of stress-reduction skills, we can empower ourselves and take control of our own relaxation.

I first became interested in stress reduction in the 1960s when I was a fairly tense young wife, and the mother of three young children. My interest in stress reduction intensified during the 10 years I worked as a senior family counselor and mediator for the Conciliation Court of Los Angeles County Superior

Court. All of my clients were divorcing parents litigating over custody of their children. Emotions and tension levels in my office rose very high. It was not unusual for clients to yell and scream at each other, cry, sob, plead, storm out of the room, or even try to punch each other. In the face of this extreme tension on a daily basis, I found it necessary to develop a repertoire of stress-reduction skills for myself so that I could remain calm, focused, and effective, no matter what was going on.

After retiring from the Court and returning to private practice, I taught the stress-reduction skills to my clients, and in the fall of 1991, I began presenting stress-reduction lectures on-board Princess Cruises.

Stress rarely comes from just one source, so the most auspicious way to combat stress is to adopt a broad, holistic approach. This requires attacking various causes of stress by a broad variety of means, all at the same time. First to be presented here are physical techniques for reducing stress, followed by reducing stress through changes in attitudes and behavior.

Physical techniques for reducing stress

The 15 physical techniques that follow are designed to offer immediate relief from stress. While practicing these techniques, maintain deep breathing, because it is through the breath that deep relaxation can be achieved. Most of these techniques are adapted from the ancient discipline of yoga, which I have been practicing for many years. I suggest you practice as many of these techniques as time allows, repeating them as often as desired. Some may appeal to you and relax you more than others.

In preparation, read through the instructions for each particular exercise several times before commencing the exercise, then follow the simple instructions and enjoy its benefits.

1. Observing the breath

Close your eyes and just observe your breath. This can be done sitting, lying, or standing. Notice your lungs filling with air and then notice the air going out. Do not attempt to regulate or slow down the breath, just observe what your breath is doing naturally. After a few minutes, your breathing will slow down on its own and you will begin to experience relaxation. You can utilize this simple exercise anytime and anywhere. No one will even detect what you are doing.

2. Counted breathing

Slowly inhale for two counts, hold your breath for two counts, exhale your breath for two counts, and hold your breath out for two counts. Repeat this pattern 20 times and experience the relaxation. Once you become proficient in this technique, try slowing down your breath even more by inhaling as you count to four, holding for four counts, exhaling for four counts, and holding your breath out for four counts.

3. The hissing breath

Take in a deep breath through your nose. Hold it in for a moment, then hiss the breath out slowly through your clenched teeth until every bit of breath is gone. Follow this exhalation with a few slow, deep breaths. Repeat this technique again twice and experience the relaxation.

4. The sponge

Lie flat on your back and close your eyes. Begin by observing your breath as in Technique #1. Next, take five counted breaths as in Technique #2. Afterward, inhale deeply and hold your breath. This time, as you exhale your breath, visualize letting go of all of the tension from your toes and feet. Inhale, hold your breath again, and as you exhale this breath, visualize letting go of all tension from your ankles and calves. Keep repeating these steps, slowly, progressing upward from your feet to your head, gradually releasing tension from each part of the body: your thighs, genital-rectal area, hips, lower back, abdomen, mid-back diaphragm, chest, upper back, shoulders, arms and hands, neck and throat, jaw and temples, eyes and forehead, nape of neck and scalp. After you have gone through your entire body, inhale deeply, hold your breath, and as you exhale this breath, feel a wave of relaxation throughout your entire body. Repeat this last relaxing breath again, then lie quietly for a few minutes, taking slow deep breaths and relaxing more deeply with each breath.

5. Visualization

Begin with Technique #4. At the end of the exercise, as you are lying there, taking slow deep breaths, imagine yourself in a peaceful and beautiful place, perhaps in a beautiful garden, or on a raft floating down a lazy river, or on a white fluffy cloud, or a quiet beach, wherever you could feel very comfortable, safe, and at peace. Now, as you take in a deep breath, imagine yourself being there and feeling comfortable, safe, and relaxed. Continue taking slow, deep breaths, allowing yourself to enjoy the relaxation. Realize that this place is yours, just a few slow, deep breaths away, and you can go there anytime you wish.

6. Scanning

Mentally scan your entire body for tense areas. As you come to an area that is tense, take a deep breath, hold it for a moment, and as you exhale the breath, release all the tension from that area. Repeat this format for all tense areas.

7. Head rolls

Sit in a comfortable position and close your eyes. Drop your head forward onto your chest. Inhale as you bring your chin around toward the right shoulder, and as you exhale, slowly bring your head back down to your chest. Next, inhale, bring your head slowly around to your left shoulder and down to your chest. Repeat this entire technique three times.

8. Shoulder shrugs

Inhale as you roll your shoulders forward, then up toward your ears and down toward your back, letting your shoulders go as you exhale the breath. Repeat this. Next, inhale as you roll your shoulders from back to front, letting your shoulders go as you exhale the breath. Repeat this.

9. Tighten and release

Inhale, tighten your entire body, hold for five counts, and release with a big sigh and hiss. Afterward, take slow, deep breaths and relax.

10. Shiatsu pressure points

To release tension in your neck and shoulders: Press in the center of your shoulders (halfway between the base of your neck and the other end of your shoulder) with your fingertips. Hold for 30 seconds, then repeat on the other side. *To relieve palpitations, insomnia, and nervousness:* Turn one hand so that your palm faces you. Press the thumbnail of your other hand into the side of your wrist where the hand and wrist join, on the side of your little finger. Hold for one to five minutes, then repeat on your other hand.

11. Tapping

Gently tap your shoulders, back, upper chest, and neck with your fingertips as you take slow, deep breaths.

12. Scalp and neck massage

Sit in a chair or in a cross-legged position on the floor. Close your eyes. Using both hands, gently massage the back of your neck and scalp, especially at the base of the neck, with your fingertips in a gentle circular motion. Take slow, deep breaths and relax.

13. Self-massage, or exchange massage

Massage your neck, head, shoulders, back, calves, and feet while you take slow, deep breaths and relax.

14. Palming

Rub your palms together until they feel warm. Cover your eyes gently with both hands, holding them there for 30 seconds. (Your elbows should be resting against your body or on a table or desk.) Repeat as you take slow, deep breaths and relax.

15. Remaining calm in a crisis

When you feel tense, anxious, or angry, and you want to calm yourself in order to handle a crisis in a clear, rational way, follow Techniques #1 and #2. Your eyes can remain open or closed, depending on the circumstances. These two breathing practices can help calm you so you can respond in a crisis with a clear head.

Meditation

Scientific research has found meditation to bring about deep states of relaxation along with many health benefits. Meditation also quiets the mind and can even bring about a state of euphoria. There are various types of meditation. The one I use is transcendental meditation, which I learned many years ago from a book titled *Transcendental Meditation*. These simple instructions are easy to follow.

Step 1. Set aside 15 to 20 minutes when you will not be disturbed. You should wait at least one hour after eating or do this one hour before eating, or you might become nauseous.

Step 2. Sit in a chair or on a couch and close your eyes.

Step 3. Begin to observe the thoughts coming into your mind. Let them come and go freely for the first one and a half to two minutes.

Step 4. Begin saying the sound, or mantra, "Oh-m-m-m-m" to yourself. Repeat this mantra as often as necessary for the remainder of the time to keep your mind free of any conscious thoughts. If your mind is blank, you need not repeat the mantra; however, if you should have any conscious thoughts, immediately repeat the mantra to keep your mind quiet and relaxed. You will find this meditation very relaxing and revitalizing.

Step 5. Practice this meditation twice daily or as often as possible.

Autogenics

Autogenics is a very easy and effective relaxation technique that can be completed in five to 10 minutes any time of the day or night. This technique was developed in the 1930s by German psychiatrist Johannes H. Schultz. I came across it in Leslie Kenton's book *Beat Stress* (Ivy Books), and have been using it often ever since. Autogenics can be used for a relaxing rest break, before retiring, and even during the night if you should wake up and have difficulty going back to sleep.

Sit comfortably or lie flat and close your eyes. Silently give yourself the following commands, and repeat each command three times, as I did here:

1. **My left arm is heavy.** My left arm is heavy. My left arm is heavy.

2. **My right arm is heavy.** My right arm is heavy. My right arm is heavy.

3. **Both arms are heavy.** Both arms are heavy. Both arms are heavy.

4. **Both legs are heavy.** Both legs are heavy. Both legs are heavy.

5. **Arms and legs are heavy.** Arms and legs are heavy. Arms and legs are heavy.

6. **Arms and legs are warm.** Arms and legs are warm. Arms and legs are warm.

7. **My breathing is slow and easy.** My breathing is slow and easy. My breathing is slow and easy.

8. **My heart rate is slow and rhythmic.** My heart rate is slow and rhythmic. My heart rate is slow and rhythmic.

9. **My solar plexus* is warm.** My solar plexus is warm. My solar plexus is warm.

10. **My forehead is cool and clear.** My forehead is cool and clear. My forehead is cool and clear.

11. **I am at peace.** I am at peace. I am at peace.

    *Just below the rib cage.

When you wish to bring yourself out of this self-hypnotic state, make two fists, then raise both arms overhead. Separate your fingers wide apart, open your eyes wide, and look at your fingers and at the ceiling.

Other physical modalities for reducing tension and anxiety

Biofeedback

Using scientifically proven biofeedback electronic instruments, a person can learn to regulate various internal processes, including heart rate, blood pressure, muscle tension, and even brain-wave activity. Gaining control over internal functions allows the recipient to relax at will and normalize stress levels.

Hypnosis and self-hypnosis

Both are scientifically proven means for inducing relaxation. Therapists with specialized training can provide hypnosis. The hypnotist psychically induces the subject into an altered state of consciousness by telling the subject to feel sleepy, drowsy, and relaxed, to breathe deeply and comfortably and go into a deep sleep. Once the subject is hypnotized, the hypnotist can give the subject directions and posthypnotic suggestions that can affect the subject's behavior in a positive way when he or she wakes.

Chiropractic

Through adjustments of the spine, alignment is improved as well as function of the nervous system. As nerve flow is enhanced, the body is revitalized and tension caused from misalignment is released.

Acupuncture and acupressure

As stress compounds in the body, vital energy pathways, or meridians, can become blocked, thus causing distress or disease. Acupuncture needles, strategically placed, or acupressure at a particular point, can reopen blocked channels and release stress. This method dates back thousands of years.

Reflexology

Stimulation of key points in the feet and body send reflective waves, or stimulation, to organs and tissues, allowing them to relax.

Massage and various sorts of body work

These modalities can be very beneficial for releasing tension from the body. For example, Heller Work practitioners, using deep tissue manipulation, systematically release deep-set tension held in the body's connective tissues. This allows freer movement, improved alignment, and an enhanced sense of well-being.

Physical exercise

Physical exercise provides a natural release from tension. Among these are sports of various sorts including stretching, walking, jogging, running, swimming, bicycling, and dancing.

Sexual release

Sexual release has long been known to lessen body tension, especially when followed by relaxing sleep or rest.

Reducing stress through change in attitudes and behavior

Certain attitudes and behaviors make life more stressful. The very nature of these attitudes and behaviors creates tension. By becoming conscious of these attitudes and behaviors and aware of the damage they cause both us and our loved ones, we can then choose to change them.

Tension-producing attitudes

Having to be perfect. If we want to feel good about ourselves and be at peace, then perfection is an unrealistic goal, because *no one* is perfect. We all have our strengths and weaknesses. This does not mean that we should not strive to improve ourselves. But we should not chastise ourselves for not being perfect. Not being perfect does not mean we are failures. A better goal to strive for is doing our very best in every situation, under whatever circumstances we find ourselves. When we learn to be our own good friend, instead of our own worst critic, we eliminate a lot of stress, and can have happier lives.

Having to be the best. An overly competitive attitude or the practice of comparing ourselves to others breeds tension. No matter how good we are, there is always someone better, richer, more beautiful, more handsome, or smarter. Only by accepting ourselves where we are now, while striving to improve, can we experience feelings of success and satisfaction.

Actually, whether we consider ourselves a success or failure is a highly subjective matter. Imagine a graduating high school class: The graduate second from the highest scholastically was miserable because he wasn't the first. He didn't get the top "A," whereas, the graduate who was second from the lowest in the class, was thrilled. She was the first one in her whole family to graduate from high school.

Strange as it may seem, a powerful affirmation to help ease us out of "having to be the best" is saying to ourselves, "I am the best, and I deserve the best." Once we feel good about ourselves, we are less apt to be concerned about having to be the best.

Having to keep up with the Joneses. Trying to compete with others costs enormous amounts of money. If we can't enjoy what we have, then it is unlikely we will be content with more, no matter how much. Satisfaction comes in being able to appreciate and enjoy what we have.

Having to be right. Everyone likes to be right. We like others to agree with our point of view. We dislike being proved wrong. When carried to extreme, however, those who have to be right tend to make others wrong. They are not often willing to consider as valid any other point of view than their own, and are not even willing to listen to another point of view. For the person who has to be right, this is bound to cause tension in all of their relationships, and for all with whom that person interacts. Relationships become especially stressful when interactions lead to power struggles between two individuals who have to be right. This is not to say that we should not have strong convictions and our own moral principles, but problems arise when we try to impose our point of view on others, without regard or respect for their rights to have their own opinions.

Tension-producing behavior patterns

Trying to control a partner. When one partner tries to control or dominate the other, tension is created between them. Eventually the dominant partner usually rebels or may leave the relationship altogether. Even if the dominated partner stays, the controlling partner is usually tense and as unhappy as the one being dominated. This makes for an uncomfortable and lonely life unless the domineering partner is willing to ease his or her controlling, dominating behavior. Then stress between partners can be reduced and the relationship can be more satisfying for both partners.

Trying to change a partner. Most people are very resistant to being changed, unless they themselves are motivated to change. So, when we try to change our partner, we are bound to meet with resistance and often hostility. This leads to frustration and unhappiness for both parties.

Julie had a very rejecting father. She married Andrew who was neither demonstrative nor affectionate. She became extremely upset with him for not being more affectionate, and kept trying to change him. The tension this created caused Andrew to withdraw and give her even less affection. A skilled counselor or therapist can help bring about balance and insight to both partners in such cases.

Trying to possess or hold onto a partner. A possessive person tends to feel insecure and unloved, even when he or she is loved. Linda was very angry when she described her possessive husband: "If I went to the market with the kids, Bob would accuse me of seeing another man. There is no other man." Possessive people fear losing their partner, so they hang on very tightly, and the tighter they hang on, the more uncomfortable their partner feels. Because of their behavior, in the end, possessive people are likely to lose the very person they are trying so hard to hang onto.

Carrying grudges. Carrying grudges against someone who hurt, slighted, cheated, betrayed, or rejected us harms only us, not the person who wronged us. Carrying grudges depletes our energy and keeps us stuck in the past. We do ourselves a big favor when we can forgive the other person. The forgiveness processes described in Chapter 7 can be very therapeutic.

Seeing yourself as a victim. When things go wrong, it is so much easier to blame our partner than ourself. The problem with this system is that, when we see ourselves as victim, we avoid taking responsibility for our choices and what happens to us. Taking total responsibility for our own behavior takes great honesty. If we had done things differently, the outcome would not have been the same.

Even in cases where one is abusing the other, it takes two people to make that relationship what it is. If one partner allows herself or himself to be abused and doesn't seek help, call the police, or leave, then that person is also responsible for the harm that is done to him or her. Continued abuse would not be possible if the abused person takes some action to stop it. In cases where a parent allows a child to be abused by the other parent and doesn't seek help and protection for the child, that parent is also responsible for the child abuse.

Process for Assessing Responsibility

The following process can assist you in examining and assessing your responsibility for events that have occurred in all of your relationships. I suggest setting aside 30 to 60 minutes for reviewing events throughout your life.

Step 1. Begin with the most recent incident in which you felt yourself to be a helpless victim, a time when you felt you were abused, taken advantage of, hurt, rejected, threatened, overworked, or treated unfairly.

Step 2. Go through the sequence that led up to this event and look at what you may have done to help cause the event or incident, such as being overly dependent or submissive, critical, unkind, unloving, sarcastic, helpless, childish, rejecting, insensitive, unprepared, domineering, possessive, insecure, impatient, unresponsive, forgetful, disorganized, irresponsible, overly extravagant, neglectful, or any other behavior that might have helped instigate or precipitate the incident or event. It may have been an unkind word or an angry look, or something you may have done or said—or not done or said—that caused your partner to feel rejected and unloved.

Step 3. Once you have completed that event, go back in time to another incident or event in which you felt yourself to be the victim. Examine that event, like an investigator, finding ways in which you were responsible for the event or situation, or ways in which you influenced the outcome of the event.

Step 4. After the second incident or event has been examined, go back in time again to another incident and another, and another, until you have gone through the major events in your life in which you felt yourself to be the victim.

To demonstrate how this process works, I will describe an incident that occurred in my own life: When I was a child of about 6 years old, an event happened with my father for which I totally blamed him. It was not until I was grown, years later, that I was able to realize how I had caused the event. What I remembered through the years was that I was sitting on my father's lap one evening when he suddenly pushed me off and shouted, "Get away from me!" This stood out in my mind as a sign that my father did not love me. I never thought about what I might have done to cause his abrupt response. I felt rejected, unloved, and sorry for myself—the classic victim. It was not until I reexamined the event in the way I have suggested that I realized what I had done to him to precipitate his throwing me off his lap.

I was playing with his hair at first and then tickling his neck and ear. Then I lifted my head and licked his ear. At the time, this might have seemed innocent, but actually it was a very seductive thing to do. His response was to get away from me as fast as he could. He did this both to protect his own integrity and to protect me. I, on the other hand, blamed him for rejecting me. Ever since I have been willing to acknowledge my part in what happens to me, I feel powerful instead of like a helpless victim.

Reducing stress through positive lifestyle changes

Even with the best of intentions, it is very difficult to achieve a life-affirming lifestyle. Our pace is often too hectic, eating habits are unhealthy, and care of our bodies is haphazard at best. Most people take better care of their cars and pets than they do of themselves. We think erroneously that our bodies will last forever, no matter what we do.

Positive lifestyle changes, such as taking periodic breaks, setting priorities, eating healthy, and keeping fit can improve health, well-being, and quality of our relationships. Following are six categories of positive lifestyle changes to consider.

Categories of positive lifestyle changes

1. Caring for your body. Providing yourself with a nourishing, wholesome diet, getting enough exercise and rest, giving up smoking if applicable, taking mini-breaks and vacations to revitalize yourself, and using stress-reduction techniques to relax.

2. Nurturing your relationships. Spending time with loved ones and friends, making a commitment to those you love, learning how to communicate and share feelings, learning how to settle disagreements and differences, and learning how to deal effectively with anger.

3. Finding satisfying work. Finding a work situation where you feel valued and stimulated, and where you receive adequate compensation for your efforts and labors.

4. Managing time efficiently. Preparing lists to help you organize errands and calls, planning out your schedule to allow for delays, avoiding overcrowding your schedule and rushing, and possibly moving closer to work or working closer to home to free up additional time.

5. Monitoring responsibilities. Saying no to those who want to dump their responsibilities on you, and taking on only what you can manage without overstraining yourself. Some people can take on more responsibility and stress than others. Listen to yourself and your own body.

6. Creating enjoyable escapes. Finding hobbies, interests, or recreational activities that give you pleasure and stimulation. These can be done alone or with loved ones or friends, and need not cost a lot of money. There is a great variety to choose from, and you can be as creative as you like.

Juggling time and energy

The problem for many of us is taking on too many commitments. We juggle work, family, home, friends, social obligations, and community service and become spread way too thin. If we can reduce our commitments even slightly and manage to schedule brief periods of time for rest, relaxation, and recreation, we lessen stress for ourselves. For those people who have a problem about taking on too many commitments, I suggest the following: Stand in front of a mirror, look yourself in the eye, and say, "No! No! No!" If you repeat this often enough, it becomes easier to say no when you need to.

Consider the following concepts and questions when evaluating what lifestyle changes you might wish to make:

➢ You aren't going to live forever.

➢ You can't take it with you.

➢ Important relationships must be nurtured.

➢ If you don't take care of yourself, no one else will.

➢ If you don't have time for some fun, what is it all for?

➢ If you do nothing to help others, what kind of person are you?

➢ If you only had six months to live, what kind of changes would you make in your life?

➢ What changes could give you satisfaction and self-fulfillment?

➢ What are your priorities?

When considering lifestyle changes

It is not an easy matter to change habits. Changes can be uncomfortable and even scary, but where health, well-being, and quality of relationships is concerned, the struggle to accomplish an important goal is worth the effort it takes. Following are eight steps to help you accomplish your goals:

1. **Become aware that a change is needed**, for example, a need to reduce cholesterol or give up smoking.

2. **State your intention.** Your intention that you want to change must be clear.

3. **Visualize** yourself in a situation where you have a choice, and visualize yourself making a beneficial choice.

4. **Make preparations for forming new habits**, for example, having healthy food on hand.

5. **Give yourself time** for new habits to take hold and for tastes to develop.

6. **Don't come down hard on yourself** if you should slip back once in a while.

7. **When possible, find a friend or support group** with similar goals you are trying to attain.

8. **No flag-waving or trying to change others.** You will naturally inspire others.

Reducing ingrained tension and anxiety

As human beings, we tend to recycle painful and stressful experiences over and over again:

> ➤ The grievances we didn't communicate.

> ➤ The situations that were never resolved.

> ➤ The feelings that were not acknowledged or understood.

> ➤ The mistakes that were made that could not be undone.

> ➤ The hurts that never healed.

> ➤ The dreams and hopes that never materialized.

Leftover business from the past adds to stress levels in the present. As a result, tension and anxiety are constant companions for most of us. We live with this level of stress, become accustomed to it, and come to believe that this is the way life has to be. But this is not the case.

Process for Reducing Ingrained Tension and Anxiety

Most of my counseling clients struggle, not only with their present relationships, but from ingrained tension and anxiety that they bring along from childhood. It is my task as therapist to help them unburden themselves. For this purpose I use a process to reduce ingrained tension and anxiety. This brings both relief and insight, because it enables individuals to completely experience what is burdening them. I have been using this powerful process for therapeutic purposes since I experienced it myself in the 1970s at a human potential movement seminar called E.S.T.

The rationale for why this process works is that when feelings and problems are experienced completely, they lose their power over us and we are free—or freer—of them. Upsetting feelings and problems stay with us so long because we resist experiencing them fully, especially unpleasant or painful experiences from childhood. We repress them or try not to think about them because they are too unpleasant or painful. As a result, they stay around to haunt us, even as adults. Much of the tension and anxiety we experience as adults is linked to childhood. The process for reducing ingrained stress enables us to be free and to live more in the present.

The benefits from this kind of work are truly amazing. The result you can expect is a clearing up or freeing up of whatever particular feeling, conflict, barrier, tension, or problem you choose to focus on or work on. The format for this process is quite structured with clear and simple instructions, and the results are extraordinary, giving both relief and newfound freedom.

Two case studies

The two case studies that follow will acquaint you with this process and allow you to experience how it works.

The case studies of Jeff and Lori that follow clearly demonstrate how ingrained tension and anxiety begins from an early age, and how the Process for Reducing Ingrained Tension and Anxiety helped rid them of tension and anxiety. In the first case study, Jeff, a young dentist, was experiencing tension and anxiety in connection with his work. In the second case study, Lori, a working mother, was under constant pressure and wasn't able to enjoy her life.

Jeff

Jeff, a tall, handsome, bright young dentist with a new practice, wife, and baby, came in for a two-hour counseling session to work on the uncomfortable feeling he was experiencing every Sunday evening in anticipation of returning back to work on Monday. His wife, Sue, was concerned about him and insisted he seek help. At my suggestion, she accompanied Jeff and sat in during Jeff's session in order to get a better understanding of what Jeff's problems were about.

Tensely, Jeff described his problem: "I think it has to do with financial survival and worrying if I'm going to make it. I worry if my patients will like me and will be pleased with my work, and also if I can handle the amount of business it takes to be successful. I worry if I don't get patients, I won't make it financially, and, if I get too many, I worry that I can handle the workload and keep them satisfied and coming back."

I briefly explained to Jeff the Process for Reducing Ingrained Tension and Anxiety, then I led him through it. As his main area of focus, he selected the tense, anxious feeling he was experiencing. He kept this in mind as he began to focus on his body sensations. He described feeling tension in his arms and shoulders, and a queasy feeling in his stomach, which he explained as: "the feeling you get if you're afraid and dreading something." The emotions he felt were fear and nervousness. I asked him to experience these emotions for a few minutes.

When asked what his behavior patterns were in connection with his tension and anxiety or how he has been dealing with his anxiety, he replied, "I don't really. I just do what I do. It doesn't really stop me from doing anything. I have these awful feelings, but you have to continue what you're doing. You have to function. I don't stop functioning. Sometimes I get a little mad when patients come late or don't show up. I take it personally if someone doesn't show or call, like it's my fault, like they weren't pleased or otherwise they wouldn't do such a thing. If they come in a couple of times and then they quit or they cancel and say they'll call back and never do, I take it personally. You lose some and you don't know why. It makes me very anxious. Sometimes I feel like calling the patient, but then you don't want to buy someone. I know I'm not supposed to take it personally, but I just like everything to run perfectly. So I don't do very well when I'm anxious."

I asked Jeff what thoughts he had about his anxiety and tension and Jeff replied, "It's something I don't like but I don't know what other way to behave. I'm just used to it. I'm always tense about one thing or another. It's like part of my life, but it's a part I don't like. It makes life miserable. I don't enjoy it. I don't even enjoy work when I'm like that. I don't want to get up in the morning and go to work. Even when I have free time, I'm preoccupied with all these problems. I'm always thinking about things and I can't get away from work, even when I'm not working. It's a burden I don't want to have.

To my question, "What is it saying way back in your mind, Jeff?" he said it was saying, "I get anxious because I'm trying to control people. I can't control everything."

Jeff's first mental image was when he was around 9. He was playing baseball in the outfield and was not paying attention. Then someone hit a ball and it just landed in his mitt. Jeff stated, "It was total luck. I shouldn't have caught the ball. I was just standing there daydreaming. I don't know what this has to do with my anxiety." He recalled always being anxious about sports. His next few images were of a difficult patient who was "draining" him; an image of himself feeling very uptight and nervous when he was running late at the office; of himself in the clinic while at dental school; not feeling very competent; and of his daughter falling, cutting her lip, and crying hysterically.

Jeff said he felt he had always been anxious and uneasy, worrying about not being good enough at sports. His parents were both very successful, and he felt uneasy. Theirs was a "hard act to follow, like trying to measure up." Jeff began to see images of his father looking at him rather disapprovingly when he felt Jeff's grades weren't good enough, or when Jeff was acting lazy. Jeff saw an image of his father telling him how easy he had it, compared to how hard he himself had it as a child. That made Jeff feel like a lazy person. The idea of being financially independent was frightening for Jeff. His fear was whether he was going to make it. Jeff saw a series of images of himself being "bailed out" of difficult situations, like when he played sick to get out of a race because he was afraid he wouldn't win. His mind flashed back to elementary school, feeling so nervous about the games and feeling inferior. Competitions made him nervous. Jeff was also nervous about a 10-kilometer run two months away.

Jeff said he was getting bored with this conversation, but I encouraged him to keep looking for additional images. He responded, "I keep seeing this one image, but I don't know how it fits in. When I was about 4, my mother was changing my clothes.

Some kids in the house were laughing at me. They all giggled and ran out of the room. I didn't have my clothes on because I cut myself and my mom was trying to fix it. I felt so embarrassed. I didn't want to go out for a long time. I was afraid to have anyone see me. Right now I keep seeing images of people who told me I can't do anything good, my brother telling me I couldn't sing, some bullies trying to beat me up, and me being scared."

Jeff was concerned he wasn't doing this process very well, but I reassured him he was doing fine. Jeff next saw an image of himself at summer camp, not going to the bathroom for days because there were no locks on the doors. He felt anxious there the entire time and couldn't wait to go home.

Jeff talked about always being shy, and he wondered when it all started. "It's like it started at a certain time, but I can't put my finger on when. I was scared to be in groups of people and scared of little girls later on. I have one image, it's really strange. It's like the image of when I thought that life was no longer fun. I was about five years old. I remember that every day was filled with fun. I used to get all these kids together and we'd play in the hills behind the house where we lived, but one day I couldn't get anyone to come out and play. Everyone was busy. I remember that was the first day I said, "I'm not having fun. Before that, every day was fun."

I commented, "School might have started," and he responded, "It must have been school. All of a sudden, none of the kids could play anymore."

Jeff's jaw was still clenched and he felt restless. He said, "It's because I'm an uptight person." He was still experiencing a feeling of anxiety and nervousness as he stated, "It's a fear of failure." He was visualizing his business folding up and he and his family living out of his car.

This brought up a feeling of sadness in Jeff, thinking of failing his family when they were counting on him. Jeff believed his fear was realistic: "Only last week I thought I was going to have to close up shop and quit, but at the very end of the week, it just sort of came alive, and then I did okay. Every week is the same thing. It's like being on the brink of disaster, but generally I seem to do okay or make a little bit above what I was expecting. I'm still on the line. It's not fictitious. I don't like feeling so anxious. It's no way to go through life worrying about every week." Way back in Jeff's mind, it was saying, "It's not good to be fearful. It's not helpful. It's not beneficial. It's not pleasant. But I'm that way for a reason. I have a fear of failure."

Jeff's mental images now were of high school football, of him spraining his ankle and not making it to the front of the line, of his coach being mad, and later of him not doing well in the game: "I wasn't quite the material they were looking for. Once, when I lost weight, the coach was really upset with me. I usually ended up sitting it out and watching everyone play, and waiting until the next game. I'm worried that my business and my practice will be the same way. Last January was bad, but I guess it was better than the year before. Every time I feel that I'm doing well, I have a bad week. It's like my life has to depend on each week. There's so much anxiety. If I have a bad week, then I worry about surviving. If I have a good week, I wonder if I can handle it. Also, what about next week? I always worry about next week. I think, 'I did well this week, but next week's going to be a disaster.' So I'm never pleased and I sort of get down on myself. It's like the coach chewing me out all over again. It's like I can't do one good thing. It's so hard to be perfect all the time."

More images from Jeff's past came to mind: He got lost at a summer camp and got into trouble for wandering off. He took money from his mother's purse and treated all of the kids in the neighborhood to ice cream and another time, donuts. He was sent to his room because he hit people. He was being chased by a big boy and was very afraid. He got into a fight with his best friend.

Jeff began to yawn, but was still experiencing a little tension in his jaw, so I had him quickly review the process again. By this time, Jeff said he was feeling drained. "I'm tired. I think it's tiring. I don't know how I put up with this tension and anxiety. I must be exhausted." Now, way back in Jeff's mind, it was saying, "It gets to me. It's very fatiguing. I shouldn't be that way. I shouldn't have to be anxious."

This time around, two more frightening images came to Jeff's mind: He was caught in a headlock by a boy while playing a game, such as hide and seek. "He was choking me and he wouldn't let go, and I couldn't get him to let go. Finally someone forced him to let go. I remember that horrible feeling. He was stronger than me at that time. I thought he was going to kill me. Also, in life-saving class, I thought someone was going to drown me. We were doing our drill where you had to rescue someone. The guy had me under water. I was struggling to come up for air. The more I struggled, the tighter his grip got. I thought I was going to drown. I finally started gouging him with my nails, and he finally let me go. But I almost drowned."

I commented, "It's life and death stuff you're talking about now."

Jeff replied, "Yeah, I was pretty scared. Both times I felt like I was very close to going under or passing out. With the guy in life-saving class, it was an accident, but the other was on purpose. He was trying to choke me."

Those were the last images Jeff saw. I suggested he take a few more minutes to experience them. After a few minutes, he and his wife left.

Two months passed before I spoke to Jeff and Sue again. Sue called to tell me the great difference she was seeing in Jeff. He was taking things much more in stride, and was much more cheerful and fun to be with. Then Jeff got on the phone and said, "I want to thank you. I'm much more comfortable around my patients now, and I think they sense this. Lately, I've been getting a lot of referrals from patients. I'm very busy. If this keeps up, I'll have a very good year. It's a good thing. Sue is pregnant again and we'll have another mouth to feed soon."

Lori

Lori, age 40, was one of the tensest counseling clients I have ever worked with. She was a single working mother who felt herself under constant pressure. Her goal was to feel freer, more at ease, and able to enjoy life with her live-in boyfriend, Rick, and her 6-year-old daughter, Stacey.

Lori's father was an alcoholic, and her mother had many nervous breakdowns, shock treatments, and was an obsessive overeater. Rick was also an overeater. He had recently been hospitalized for 35 days for this problem, but afterward, he was still either abstaining or bingeing. Aside from his eating problem, Lori described their relationship as good, even though they were each very different. Things didn't seem to bother Rick the way they bothered her.

Lori wanted to feel less pressured and more at peace. She felt overwhelmed and torn in all directions, unable to give enough to her boyfriend and her daughter, and be a homemaker, and a nurse. She had always been very active and busy, so different from her mother who spent most of her time in bed, flat on her back.

When I led Lori through the Process for Reducing Ingrained Tension and Anxiety, her main focus was on feeling overwhelmed. She felt a generalized tension through her entire body. I asked her to experience that body sensation for a few moments. Lori's main emotion was fear. All her life, she saw her parents being so sick. There was no way she wanted to be like them, and she was afraid she would be. She was irritable and impatient with her own daughter: "I only relate to her like a drill sergeant."

Lori explained, "I'm so overwhelmed myself, I have to give orders to get everything done. I push myself to get one more thing done. I feel nervous and jumpy, like there's a cloud over my head. There is so much to do. There's a heaviness I feel. I guess I'm really rigid. It's hard to keep it up, and I'm a perfectionist. I think I shut people out, and I prefer things over people. It's easier to relate to things than to people."

Lori commented that Rick wanted to go away occasionally for weekends, but she preferred to stay home and do things like clean out the garage. More and more, she wanted to stay home.

She was becoming more and more anxious about letting Stacey go places with friends, afraid that something might happen to her. She wondered why she couldn't just relax and let it flow instead of pushing herself.

Lori thought that her behavior was extreme and unhealthy. She was worried that it was getting worse, and it was detrimental to her relationships with Stacey and Rick. Way back in her mind, the words were, "You better get rid of this tension or you'll be in bad shape."

Her first mental image was of herself as a student in college, overwhelmed by all of the reading she had to do. During her first few years of nursing, she didn't feel overwhelmed. She had no responsibility then and no children. "Today I don't give as much. I can't be that much to everyone. When first I was married, we had a tiny house and my former husband, Jim, was messy. I was frustrated, but I don't remember feeling that driven. After Stacey was born, I gained all this responsibility and I lost my ability to relax and have fun."

While Lori was growing up, much of the responsibility fell on her. She saw an image of herself at the age of 9 or 10, standing over her mother. "She's in bed depressed. I'm angry and yelling at her to get up and be my mother. When she was sick, my dad would stop drinking, and when she was well, he'd start drinking again. I buried myself in my work and church activities." Lori was valedictorian of her high school graduation class and graduated from college with honors. Then she met Jim and married him. After Stacey was born, she began to feel tremendous pressure. Lori remarked, "I was a mother now. I couldn't be everything. Some fun in life went away. I didn't want children. Jim convinced me that things would work out, so I decided to have a baby. I lost something of me."

Lori saw an image of herself with Stacey, when Stacey was a baby, and then at around 2½ years old. She commented, "I had to do so much and be so much. I see an image of myself as a new mother, going through the motion of being a mother and a homemaker. Now I see myself as a little child of 2 or 3. I can't see my mother, but I have a vague sense she's somewhere around. I'm seeing my mother crying a lot, with dark glasses. Her face is red. It worried me. I was scared. She wasn't strong enough to be my mother."

I commented, "Is that why you have to be so strong?"

Lori responded immediately, "Yeah. If I stop and relax, I could get sucked into being like them." Lori was still feeling mild tension in her body, but not as intense as before. She experienced a feeling of sadness and then fear came over her. "It seems like I pinpointed the acute stage to when Stacey was born, then I tapped into all of the serious parts and left the carefree parts behind. I think I need to find a way to allow myself to have time that isn't productive. Rick says I don't know how to have fun. I have to let go of the cloud over me."

By this point, Lori's hands were beginning to relax and her breathing was getting deeper. "I'm seeing images of what I want to see, myself on the couch reading a book, in the pool on a float, talking and walking. I'm wishing for a feeling of contentment, of being relaxed and happy wherever I am. I've known people like that and I admire that."

Lori was feeling very relaxed now. While her eyes were still closed, I talked to her about her not having a healthy model for being a mother, about the pain of being a child and receiving so little comfort, and about her becoming a drill sergeant in order to survive. Lori had been afraid to let her guard down and show her soft side. There had been too much fear, anger, and rage left inside of her.

During the next session, Lori worked on her fear. As she walked into my office, she reported the progress she had made. "A couple of times this weekend I sat down and watched TV with Stacey. I just decided not to do any work that day. It was fun." Then her face grew sad as she added, "I was thinking from last time how serious I became after Stacey was born. I felt sad that something so wonderful as having a child could be that way."

I commented, "Your having a child brought up the pain from your own childhood."

Lori responded, "When Stacey has problems, it's hard for me. I hook into it like I'm a kid again. I have a lot of fears. Stacey has a stern teacher and I can't talk to her without crying. It's a hard time for me."

During this session, Lori worked on her fear, using the Process for Reducing Ingrained Tension and Anxiety. She described a sinking feeling, her body on alert, ready to run from some catastrophe about to occur. That was why she wanted to stay home. It was safer there. For many years she had been having scary dreams of being up on high precipices or scaffolding; recently she had had a dream that the atom bomb had dropped and she wouldn't be with Stacey.

All of her muscles were tense as she remembered feeling very afraid when her mother was sick. She was about 4 or 5 years old. "I would cry. I didn't know what was going on." Lori was experiencing a lot of fear now and I asked her not resist it. She had been holding onto this fear all these years. She thought her fear was a weakness she had gotten from her mother. Way back in her mind it was saying, "My fears are real, and they're standing in my way."

At this point, Lori's mind was blank and she was feeling no emotions. She said, "I must have a block. Fear is normal."

I commented, "Yes, fear is normal, especially when a child feels all alone and senses her parents' fears and sees her mother out of control. You had to become a parent to your parents."

Lori's mind flashed on an image of her sister, Connie, as a child, being afraid; she next saw an image of Connie's 2-year-old daughter crying as she stood over Connie. Connie had attempted suicide with an overdose of sleeping pills. She had recovered physically, but not emotionally. Lori commented, "I was always afraid of being like her, taking drugs and being like a zombie."

Lori's next image was of the morning of the big earthquake in Northridge in 1994, when her bed moved across the room. As she remembered this, a rush of fear came over Lori as she thought about how awful it would be if anything were to happen to her. "Who would take care of Stacey?" It was very painful for Lori to think about this. I asked her not to hold this feeling back. She saw a mental image of Stacey in danger and of her not able to help her. Once, Stacey had an accident and had hurt her knee badly. When Lori arrived home from work, Rick was taking care of her. Lori felt terrible she wasn't there too. Lori didn't like to think of these things. "I can see Stacey somewhere far away with a stranger and her not being able to contact me, and me not knowing where she is. I feel afraid. There are so many horrible people who might abuse children." There were tears in her eyes.

After the process, and with her eyes still closed, I told Lori that I wanted her to begin to feel very compassionate for that little girl inside of herself, who had needed parents to comfort her, hold her, reassure her, wipe away her tears, be available, and love her. They weren't there. I introduced the notion of her learning to become a good and nurturing parent, to herself and to her daughter. "At times, the world can seem like a very scary place to a child," I told her, "even with a mother there to hold you and comfort you. You didn't have that. You have become a good parent in spite of the fact that you had to raise yourself."

Lori returned for a third session. She announced that the pressure seemed to have lightened. "I don't feel that weight all the time. I'm able to interact more freely with Rick and Stacey. It's such a relief. I keep waiting for the tension to come back."

I explained to Lori, "It won't have the same intensity again. What do you want to work on today?"

Lori replied, "On my depression. There's so much in the world that's depressing. It was hard coming here today."

I commented, "Hopelessness isn't a new feeling for you." She nodded, and she worked intensely during the session on her abiding feeling of depression and hopelessness that had become a part of her life since early childhood. Lori has tried all her life, consciously and unconsciously, to push these feelings aside, because she saw what happened when her mother gave in to these feelings. Lori had resolved not to give in to hers.

This time as Lori began the Process for Reducing Ingrained Tension and Anxiety, she was able to experience her feelings of hopelessness, sadness, powerlessness, and anger toward her parents. She saw images of the utter hopelessness of her childhood: Her mother lying in bed in a dark room; her father in bed passed out; and her sister, Connie, just sitting in a chair. She reviewed images of her own nightmarish dreams; her fear of the atom bomb dropping and her not being with Stacey; and frustrating and depressing images of her mother struggling with overeating, her father and Rick struggling with being overweight. Lori stated, "I hate the super-awareness I have, and I wish I could put blinders on and not see things."

Lori was feeling drained as she reviewed the process. She said thoughtfully, "I think my feeling of hopelessness touches almost every part of my life." Now, way back in her head, it was saying, "There really is hope."

This time around, Lori saw images of herself just lying still, of she and Stacey having a good time, of a pretty green meadow, and of horses running about free. While her eyes were still closed, I explained, "To children, the universe is what they see going on in their own family. For you, your world was a very depressing place, and these feelings have remained with you. It has been especially hard for you to experience that sadness. You were afraid you would become like your mother. Lori, you are not like your mother. You are strong and you have a will to survive."

Lori replied, "I'm ready to dump this sadness. I'm tired of it."

I told Lori that this involves forgiveness and I explained how to do the forgiveness process (as explained in Chapter 7).

The last I heard from Lori was a brief note: "Thank you, Florence. I'm much lighter these days. It's a new kind of life for me. I am learning how to enjoy myself and my family. I have not felt tense or depressed for many months."

Preparatory steps before beginning this process

Most of you will be able to do this process on your own or with the help of your partner, a friend, or a loved one. Or you may prefer to ask a mental health professional to lead you through it for added emotional support. Before beginning this process, I suggest the instructions be read and followed very carefully.

A word of caution: Anyone with a history of psychiatric problems, suicidal tendencies, emotional instability, or taking tranquilizers or antidepressant medication *should not* do this process on their own without first consulting a licensed mental health professional.

Step 1. Select a time and place to do the process where you will be totally undisturbed for 90 minutes. Because this process is quite intense, it is best to allow time afterward to relax and rest.

Step 2. Decide whether you prefer to do the process on your own or with someone to assist you. Select a friend, loved one, counselor, or therapist to help you. The main drawback to doing this alone is that you might fall asleep and not be able to complete the process. This has happened to me, especially if I attempt to go through the process when I am lying down or am extremely tired. If you do try it on your own several times and are not successful in completing the process, I suggest you find someone to assist you. Then you will not be able to fall asleep, because your coach will be leading you through the process, and you will be describing what you are experiencing. It is extremely important that you complete the process to reap its full benefits.

Step 3. Select from the following list a particular main focus you wish to work on:

> ➤ *A body sensation, or a feeling in your body* that is uncomfortable and that you want to get rid of. This feeling could be generalized body tension or tightness and a holding pattern in a particular part of the body.

> ➤ *An emotion or feeling* that is pervasive and troublesome, such as anger, anxiety, frustration, fear, guilt, impatience, competitiveness, jealousy, sadness, or depression.

> ➤ *A behavior pattern* that is troublesome, such as putting yourself down; putting others down; not being able to communicate feelings;, dominating others; allowing others to dominate you, abuse you, or intimidate you; flying off the handle; having temper tantrums; or any inappropriate, self-defeating, or self-destructive behavior.

> ➤ *A thought, belief, or basic attitude* that you want to be rid of, such as, "I'm no good," "Men can't be trusted," "Women can't be trusted," "Nobody cares about me," "I'm always the victim," or "I need to be taken care of."

> ➤ *A mental image from the past* that is recurring and distressing that you want to be free of, such as a sad or frightening image from childhood or adulthood.

Take your time to decide what your focus is going to be before you begin this process. If you are having difficulty choosing between two main focus areas, select the one that is weighing most heavily on you and stay with the focus you have selected.

Step 4. Once you have selected your focus area, sit in a comfortable position with your arms and legs uncrossed, and your eyes closed.

Instructions for the process

There are five phases to this process. Each phase should be completed before moving on to the next phase.

Phase I. Focus on your body sensations. Keeping in mind the main focus area you have chosen to work on, become aware of body sensations. This could be tension in certain parts of your body, a sick or nervous feeling in your stomach, an uncomfortable or restless feeling, and so on. Your task during Phase I is to observe and experience any and every body sensation, noticing how these sensations become more or less intense or disappear as you focus on them. If someone is working with you during the process, describe to that person what you are experiencing. After approximately five to seven minutes, move on to Phase II.

Phase II. Focus on your emotions. Keeping your main focus area in mind, observe and experience whatever emotions come up, such as anger, sadness, fear, frustration, and so on. You might experience several emotions, first one, then another, then another. Experience each emotion as fully as possible. If someone is working with you during the process, describe what you are experiencing to that person. In approximately seven to 10 minutes, move on to Phase III.

Phase III. Focus on your behavior patterns. Keeping your main focus area in mind, examine all of the ways you respond and the ways you deal with the main focus area you are working on. For example, if you are working on a feeling of anger, examine what you do when you feel that anger. Examine all of your various responses and behavior patterns in connection with your main focus before you move on to Phase IV. If someone is working with you on the process, describe all these behavior patterns to that person as they occur to you.

Phase IV. Focus on your thoughts. Keeping your main focus area in mind, reflect on all of your thoughts, beliefs, and attitudes connected with this. Let your thoughts come one after the other until you run out of thoughts. If someone is working with you on the process, relate all of your thoughts to that person. Then move on to Phase V.

Phase V. Ask yourself, "What words do I hear way back in my head about this?" Listen to the first words that come to mind, even if they seem silly or unrelated. Repeat these words over and over again in your mind, like a bell ringing them out over and over again.

Phase VI. Focus on your images from the past. Still keeping your main focus area in mind, during Phase VI allow images from the past to come into your mind, as if your mind is a blank TV screen. Watch each image from the past appear, experience yourself there, and then let the image go. Keep the images coming, one after the other. Do not reject or censure any of them, even if they don't seem related. They are all related in some way and should be experienced. If someone is assisting you with the process, describe all of these images as thy occur to that person. When the images stop coming, then review the process beginning with Phase I.

Review. Briefly review all of the phases, skipping Phase III. Give special attention to what you are hearing way, way back in your mind in Phase V and also to any additional images in Phase VI. If you have someone assisting you, relate all this material to that person as it happens. Some release is usually experienced by this point. In this case, consider this the end of the process. Occasionally it is necessary to review the process again briefly in order to complete the process and experience the release.

Even after you come to the end of this process, additional material may continue to come to mind during the remainder of that day and into the next day. Observe your feelings, thoughts, and images, experience them, and let them go as you go on about your life.

What you can expect afterward

The main focus you worked on will most likely not be as pressing a problem for you again. This will free you to grow and work on other issues or problems as they come up. We are very complex creatures, and there is really no limit to the work we can do on ourselves or our potential for growth and expansion. You may begin working on depression, and afterward experience the anger that was underneath. Then, next time, work on the anger. When you work on the anger, then fear or feelings of past hurt or rejection may come to the surface to be explored and resolved. Each time you work on a troublesome feeling, body sensation, attitude, or behavior pattern, you will reap the benefits of the work that you have done.

Leading yourself through this process

In order to demonstrate how it is possible to lead oneself through this process, I taped myself while working on my anxiety about earthquakes. This example gives a vivid illustration of how it would be for you to lead yourself through the process. I focused on my anxiety about earthquakes. I am a rational person who prides herself on not being easily frightened, but the devastating earthquake in Mexico City in 1985, which killed approximately 7,000, triggered an old fear of mine and I decided to work on it.

I believe it is natural to have a certain amount of fear and dread of natural disasters, such as earthquakes, especially when one lives in the Los Angeles area. I think it is wise to be prepared by having food, water, medical supplies, and blankets handy. I also know that some of my anxiety is tied to the fear of earthquakes that I experienced as a child. A very big earthquake occurred the same year I was born: Half of the elementary school was demolished by the earthquake, and my mother never stopped talking about. I utilized the Process for Reducing Ingrained Tension and Anxiety to help me work through this fear. Below is the transcription of my taped experience as I led myself through this process.

I am closing my eyes and sitting in a relaxed position. During Phase I of the process, I focused my body sensations in connection with my fear of earthquakes: "I am feeling a slightly sick feeling in my stomach and a little shakiness in my chest. I feel throbbing in my temples, and my heart is pounding. My stomach feels a little nauseous. My shoulders feel tight, and I feel tension around my ankles, in my temples, and in my head."

During Phase II of the process, I experience my emotions in connection with my fear of earthquakes: "So far I'm not able to really feel the fear. Ah, I'm starting to feel afraid a little bit now, a little frightened feeling, sort of an insecure feeling. I'm beginning to get in touch with some fear now. I'm feeling it in my head. I'm thinking about that big earthquake. It's really scary. Danger. Danger. I'm starting to feel some sadness now. What if I were to die, or my family, or my loved ones and friends and other people were to die? I'm feeling like I'm losing someone. I just thought of my little grandkids. I want them to be safe. I feel grief, like I'm grieving for people who would be lost. A friend of mine has family in Mexico City and she was so upset after the big earthquake. She didn't get any word from her family for two weeks after the earthquake, then she found out that they were safe. All that time she thought maybe they were dead. I empathized with her. I'm feeling grief and sadness now and a real fear of being injured, having my body crushed under the house, or the roof caving in and crushing my ribs or breaking my bones."

I then shift to Phase III of the process. I examine my behavior patterns in connection with my fear of earthquakes. I ask myself what I do, what I say, and how I act or behave when I feel afraid of earthquakes. "I usually don't think about earthquakes, but I saw pictures of the earthquake in Mexico City on TV. I heard people talking more and more about a coming earthquake. I tried to put it out of my mind and tell myself that it's not going to happen now. Maybe sometime, but not necessarily now. At times I think of moving away from California. When I hear people talking about an earthquake, I think I should get some things ready and be prepared, or I just put it out of my mind. I usually deny that it's going to affect me or my loved ones. It's going to be somewhere else, some other time, like 50 or 100 years from now. I deny that it's going to happen or that it could happen at all. When I feel really scared, I feel like moving away from the city. When I am afraid, I talk to myself. I say, 'Oh, Flo, stop that. You're not going to live forever anyway. So just stop worrying about it.'"

During Phase IV of the process, I explore my thoughts in connection with my fear of earthquakes: "Maybe I'm really hiding my head in the sand like an ostrich. I think of moving away, going where it's safe. But where? Even in places that seem safe, there's something scary and dangerous. I think I shouldn't worry because it won't do any good anyway. Worrying never does any good anyway. I think I should do something in terms of preparedness to get some food, medication, and bandages lined up, and blankets and water. That's what they are suggesting in the schools. I just think I shouldn't be nervous and worried about it. I'm just worrying for no reason. Even if it happens, what's the good of worrying? Somehow I think I should be above worrying about this. I don't like feeling afraid of anything. I feel angry with myself for being afraid. I should never be afraid of anything. Invincible Flo! Strong and brave and never afraid!

"My mother was always afraid, and I don't like being afraid. She used to have nightmares and scream about the bombings in London during World War I. The world is a very insecure place. It's always been this way. It's not worse now than it was then, except maybe for the A-bomb possibility, just greater numbers of people could die. Invading hordes used to ride into a country and rape and mutilate and kill people in all the ages. It's always been like that. I wish the world were a safer place for all people, peaceful and secure. I don't want to be afraid. I want to be courageous."

After my thoughts stopped coming, I asked myself what was I hearing way, way, way back in my head about my fear? "It is saying, 'I can get killed. I can get killed. I can get killed from an earthquake. I can get killed. I can get killed.'" I let it say what it is saying over and over again in my mind.

During Phase VI, I look at images from the past: "I see myself as a young child in my parent's home, afraid of the dark. I wouldn't even go to the bathroom by myself if it was dark. I made someone take me. I was very much afraid of Frankenstein and Dracula, afraid to watch scary movies, and I still am. I avoid them. I just flashed on Alfred Hitchcock's *Psycho*. This lady was in the shower and suddenly this madman comes in and axes her. I'm frightened of fast, violent acts, whether it's earthquakes or someone murdering someone, without any warning, without anything that anyone can do. I have that powerless feeling right now, as I'm talking about this. I see an image of myself standing in front of my elementary school. Half of the building was old and half was new, built after the earthquake. My mother told me that if the earthquake had occurred during school hours, a lot of children would have died. I went to school in this building every day, and what my mother said frightened me.

"My mind is blank now, except I see an image of a hen with little chicks following behind and mother hen spreading her wings over the chicks for safety. I see a mother taking care of her little kids."

I then review this process, starting with my body sensations again: "I have a slightly upset feeling in my stomach and slight tension in my neck and shoulders. I feel a little throbbing in my stomach. I feel slightly fearful. My head is throbbing a little."

Reviewing Phase II, I am not experiencing any emotions, so I move on to Phase III and examine my thoughts and attitudes: "Well, I think I have just cause for being afraid of earthquakes because they are very dangerous. I also think that something has triggered my fears. I don't usually worry like this. It's surprising that I haven't noticed my fear all these years. This fear must have been lying dormant. Most of the time I am not afraid of these things, or of anything much. I think that I'll get over this. I'm not going to be dwelling on it. I don't want to be dwelling on it."

In reviewing Phase V again, I ask myself, "What is it saying way back in my head? It's saying, 'It's not safe, but it's okay. It's not safe, but it's okay. It'll be all right, Flo. You'll be all right. One way or another, you'll be all right. You don't have to be afraid. You don't have to be afraid. You don't have to be afraid. It's okay. It's okay. It's okay not to be afraid.'"

Last of all, reviewing Phase VI, I look at more images from the past: "Now, it's a blank but I'll wait a little. I see myself as a child running in the tall weeds. I always had very much fun doing that. I'm seeing myself being very free. I loved being outside. My sister told me that I never wanted to come in. All I wanted to do was play. I remember being on top of the jungle-gym, really high up, swinging by my knees. I was very tomboy-ish. I see an image of myself climbing trees. I love the outdoors. I can see myself being very comfortable in the world like the Indians, living on the land close to the earth. I see myself feeling secure in the world. I see myself planting flowers. I feel very grounded and not afraid."

Since I did this process many years ago, I have not been distressed by the fear of earthquakes. Now I look at the situation through adult eyes and I am better able to deal with the situation in a realistic and problem-solving mode. Lately, I have experienced a few earthquakes and I have been taking them well in my stride.

10-Step Stress Release Process

After having experienced the Process for Reducing Ingrained Tension and Anxiety, I suggest you use this 10-Step Stress Release Process whenever tense or anxious situations arise. This process takes approximately 30 to 45 minutes to complete and will give both emotional release and perspective into your circumstance and difficulty. This process is best done while sitting in a quiet place with your eyes closed (opening your eyes only to read instructions for next step). Read through the instructions carefully before commencing this process. The process can be done on your own or with your partner, friend, or therapist leading you through the steps.

Step 1. Focus on the particular situation that is causing you tension or anxiety. Ask yourself, "What am I experiencing and feeling?"

Step 2. Examine what events or circumstances have triggered your anxiety and tension.

Step 3. Search for other stresses or pressures that are adding to your feeling the way you do.

Step 4. In the past, under what circumstances have you felt this way or felt similarly?

Step 5. What decisions or resolutions did you make at that time to avoid pain or embarrassment?

Step 6. How are the decisions or resolutions you made then affecting your present behavior and your life?

Step 7. What is the worst thing that could happen to you now in connection with this? Would you survive?

Step 8. What can you do to correct or improve this situation for yourself? Think over your alternatives, and formulate a plan.

Step 9. Create a healing affirmation for yourself: one or two short sentences that will affirm your strength to be able to handle the situation, circumstance, illness, or problem that is upsetting you. For example: "I have the strength to overcome this situation. I will be stronger afterward."

Step 10. Repeat your affirmation over and over to yourself often during the next few days, and repeat this process as often as needed. See yourself as a growing person who learns from past experiences. If, in your particular case, you are not getting the relief and results you need, seek professional help.

CHAPTER 5

Past
Effects
Present

We like to think of ourselves as free agents operating in the world, fresh each day. But actually we are a composite of everything that has happened to us in the past. Our brains record everything we experience, and our bodies hold tension from past physical and emotional traumas. Troubling memories and feelings stay with us and effect our actions and decisions without our even realizing it.

When stressful problems arise in the present, we bring along certain feelings, thoughts, and experiences from the past that compound the issues, and often make resolution of these problems more difficult. The dragging along of excess baggage from the past weighs us down and confounds us. Even if no problems are yet apparent and both partners think they're doing fine, eventually, all of each partner's issues will come up, especially traumas from childhood.

As adults we are capable of resolving problems and of meeting most challenges. It is often remnants of the little child inside each one of us that causes us to feel insecure and put doubts in our minds about our abilities and capabilities. This was the case with Jim and Judy who came to see me because of their anxiety over Jim's career change. Much of their anxiety and doubts stemmed from childhood.

Jim and Judy married two years ago. They both worked in the same orthopedic doctor's office doing physiotherapy, and had managed to save up enough money for a down payment on a small home. Next year they hoped to start a family. Judy was content with how things were going before Jim went into real estate one month prior to our meeting. Jim had decided to go into real estate because he felt insecure about the future. Once they had a baby, he would be the sole provider for a while, and this was scary to him. To prepare himself for that time, Jim studied real estate, got his license, and took a full-time job in a real estate office. He also planned to work part-time as a physiotherapist.

Judy was apprehensive about Jim's going into real estate. It would be months before he would make any money. In the meantime, she would have to support both of them.

During the first session, I led Jim through the Process for Reducing Ingrained Tension and Anxiety (described in Chapter 4), while Judy listened. During the second session, I led Judy through the process while Jim listened. The results were that both of them worked through much of their anxiety and were freer to deal with the realities of the problems they now had to face.

During Jim's session, he explored the roots of his anxiety regarding changing careers. During the first phase of this process, I asked him to focus on his body sensations in connection with his career change. Jim said he felt tension in his neck and shoulders and a sick feeling in his stomach. When

I asked him to focus on images from the past, Jim described times when he felt afraid or insecure as a young child: "I'm looking down the hall. It's dark. I'm kind of afraid of what's in the hall. No one's home. I know no one's there, I just think someone might be. I was about 8 or 9."

In the next image, Jim described that he was 6 years old and on a trip: "It's kind of dark. I'm afraid of all the new things I'm seeing. I don't feel comfortable. It's not like home. I don't feel I really have a home. We move all the time, and I don't like the houses. We sold our house. We're going somewhere. I don't know where it is. I don't like the new school either. They made me write in these spaces, a certain height, and I couldn't really do it. They thought I was stupid because I couldn't do it. I never learned how to write right. It's because they were mean."

Jim was feeling very sad as he continued. "I feel very small, very tiny. I don't want to leave. I feel good there. They keep making me leave and do something. Do something, do something. I'm really tiny in my mother's arms. I feel warm and I don't want to go anywhere, but my mother is making me go somewhere. Everything feels jarring. I feel so comfortable I don't want to leave. Why can't I stay? There's always been demands on me to do things right. I just want to sit. I'm very tired. I've worked really hard doing everything that's been demanded of me."

When I asked Jim to focus again on his body sensations, he remarked, "I don't have any tension anymore. I feel good. Very relaxed. Surprisingly relaxed. I feel like a different person, more like the real me. My body feels good. I haven't felt this good in a long time."

When asked about his thoughts regarding his anxiety now, Jim replied, "I think it goes back a long way. It's based on expectations I have of myself. Real estate is something new, something I don't know how to do. I just need to learn how to do it my own way. I'm mad that I've always had to conform to live in this world. I've never felt entirely comfortable, but I have felt more comfortable these last couple of years, because I feel I'm developing into who I really am."

"This new career thing pushes me back a little bit into the past where I don't know how to do something. It's like I have to learn how to do it the way other people do it, like I've had to do all my life. I did it with physiotherapy, and with everything I know how to do. Now I want to develop my own way."

Jim said he was feeling less insecure regarding beginning his career in real estate. "I'm going to go through a little bit of learning process and then I'm going to be great at it. That's all. I'm looking forward to it, and to the adventure of what it will bring."

When I asked Jim what it was saying way back in his head now, he said it was saying, "You can do it. You can do it. You can do it." He then commented, "All my life I've always had this clash between my mom telling me, 'You can do it,' and my dad telling me, 'You can't do it. You missed the boat. You're too late.' Now he doesn't remember saying it. In some odd way, he also motivated me. Now I feel I can do it."

One concern Jim still had was that although Judy had always supported him in what he wanted to do before he went into real estate, now she wasn't. "I have to do it myself. I'm going in a direction she doesn't really know. I don't know how she feels about it. I think she's afraid. She's not sure she wants me to do real estate, so I have to sneak off and try to make it myself. I feel helpless, like I used to feel. I need help. I need her support."

As this process came to a close, I asked Jim to focus once more on images from the past. Jim saw a mental image of his yoga teacher: "He's helping me do a head stand when I know I can't do it. Now he's lifting up my legs so I can see how to do it. Then later I'm doing it on my own."

After completing the process, Jim said he was glad he went through it. I spoke to him while his eyes were still closed: "Jim, I want to tell you the same thing your mother used to tell you: You can do it. You can do it. You can do anything you really want to do. The change to real estate will either work out really well for you, or you will do something else. This is not the end of the story. You're trying something new now, and everything new is scary. You will see how it all turns out, and you have my best wishes."

The following week, as I prepared to lead Judy through the Process for Reducing Ingrained Tension and Anxiety, Judy told me that she was feeling less anxious regarding Jim's shift into real estate because he would be doing physiotherapy part-time to help pay their bills. In addition, during the previous week, he had sold his first house, so already she saw that he could be successful. Judy said the main focus she wanted to work on during this session was the tension in her back and shoulders, related to Jim's transition into real estate.

During the first portion of the process when she focused on emotions, Judy said she felt afraid. I encouraged her to experience her fear. As she experienced her fear, she explained: "I'm afraid that I won't see him. He'll be working on the weekends. It isn't that I need him around all the time. It's just that I want to see him. My feelings are hurt. I don't even know why I feel that way."

Next, Judy experienced sadness: "I don't think I like change very much, even though it always seems to be going on. I'm afraid if I relax, everything will fall apart. Jim is probably going through a lot more than I am, so I want him to think I'm okay. He came home late the other night with all this extra pressure on him, and he had to work on trying to relieve the tightness in my back. I feel bad that this is happening."

I reflected back her feelings: "So you think you're a burden and you mustn't share your own feelings or needs with him right now, because he needs your strength not your concerns right now, is that it?"

Judy agreed. When I asked her to focus on her thoughts in connection with Jim's career change, she stated, "At first I didn't even take him seriously regarding the real estate, so I didn't really support him. I'm afraid he'll drive himself like most men. I don't think it's good for them, you know, the heart attack syndrome. I don't want to see Jim do that. He never thinks he has enough. He has to have more, and I think that's unhealthy. I'm very satisfied with what we have. He tends to push himself. He doesn't even know why he's doing it. He might get hard and callused in that business.

"The other side of the coin is that I'd love to have more money, and have the freedom that goes with that. So I feel guilty having those thoughts."

When I asked Judy to focus on images from the past in connection with Jim's career change, the first mental image Judy saw was of herself selling life insurance about eight years earlier. She re-experienced that sense of uneasiness of not knowing what she was doing, and of doing what she was told instead of what she felt was right: "I remember my manager telling me, 'Oh, when you do this, you're going to get your own office with that beautiful view.' The salespeople in that office looked like they were dead, and I thought, I don't want that. They hated what they were doing."

Next, Judy saw the image of herself at another sales job, being pushy, hard, and obnoxious: "Ugh! But I was a top salesperson there. I guess I think that's what Jim will have to be. I was phony. I wore these silk dresses and I had on those phony nails, because that's what everybody did there. It was part of the game. I was plastic. I did it for acknowledgment, not for myself. When I went into sales, I started coming into my own power, which I had never had before. One boss I had was a slave driver and I worked for next to nothing for him."

Judy next saw an image of herself back in third grade. She had been picked by her teacher out of the whole class for something she had made: "I remember how creative I used to be. And you know, during those years in sales, I lost a lot of my creativity."

The next few images were of Judy as a young child, 6 or 7: "I used to walk on the side of my house and look at this hole in the wall. These birds used to go there and nest. I used to sit there all day and watch the little birdies coming through the hole in the wall, and then they went away. I was starting to grow tall and I felt really awkward. I had really big feet and my mom made me wear these really ugly shoes. There was a big wall near my neighbor's house with honeysuckle growing all over it. We used to go and cut honeysuckle and go underneath the honeysuckle and hide."

Judy commented, "This doesn't make sense."

I assured her that all of these images were related. When Judy reviewed the process, the tension between her shoulders was almost gone, and she was feeling quite relaxed. She kept seeing a fence that she used to crawl over when she was a kid. "You know, it was really tall for me to crawl over, and my mommy would yell at me about going over it, but I always did it anyway. And I was always afraid when I was doing it, too. So I guess I really like a challenge, or I wouldn't have crawled over that fence all the time. I wish the fence wasn't there for me to climb over. Why couldn't I just be lazy and not even see the fence?"

Judy added, "Right now I feel a bit stronger about this whole thing with Jim. I know that everything will work out." Now, way back in Judy's mind, it was saying, "It's a good thing."

As the process came to a close, the last images Judy saw were of her grandfather, sitting by the hour patiently drawing pictures with her, or showing her how to garden, and of herself patiently baking chocolate cakes and cream puffs for a whole day, when she was the only one who liked to eat them."

By the time Judy completed the process, she reported that the tension in her back and shoulders and her anxiety and fear were gone.

This process helped Jim and Judy let go of past anxiety and accept the challenge of a new and exciting adventure. As it turned out, Jim sold six houses during the first six-month period he spent in real estate and earned what he would have earned working full-time in physiotherapy. But after this period, Jim decided he preferred doing physiotherapy over real estate because of the dog-eat-dog attitude and lack of client loyalty. He went back to doing physiotherapy full-time and worked in real estate on the side to earn extra money. Jim considers what he learned in real estate during those six months exceedingly valuable.

Much of Jim's and Judy's present anxiety stemmed from their experiences and memories from childhood. As they re-experienced these memories in adulthood, much of their anxiety regarding the present and future fell away. As with Jim and Judy, most of us also carry painful memories from childhood that limit us in ways we are not even aware. Therefore, it is well worthwhile to explore the roots of our anxiety and free ourselves from its power over us. Through this work, we are then freer to view our lives through adult eyes and to sense life's endless possibilities.

CHAPTER 6

Handling Specific Problems

The problems presented in this chapter cover a wide range of difficult, complex, and perplexing situations that many couples face. Many of the situations discussed here appeared in my weekly column, titled "For Better or Worse," in the early 1980s. My responses to each specific situation are *not* intended as cure-alls. In each case, my goal is to offer insight, suggestions, and alternatives to consider. Many of my responses should be considered merely a first step toward improving a difficult situation, many of which may require professional help to resolve.

Lack of love and affection

Lora stated sadly, "I've been married for 17 years with no love or affection from my husband. I still love him, and I keep hoping he'll change. He refuses to go for counseling. I try so hard to be a good wife. I can't understand why he doesn't love me."

I explained my perspective: "His not being affectionate with you does not necessarily mean he doesn't love you. Some individuals find it difficult to demonstrate affection, even when they do love someone, especially if they did not receive much affection as children. There can be other reasons why he isn't affectionate with you. Perhaps he is angry with you about something that happened, even years ago, or is dissatisfied with his life in general. Sometimes, withholding affection stems from disappointment in the sexual relationship. Ask him if he is satisfied in this area and, if not, what might help him feel better about this. I suggest you tell him that your needs for affection and love are not being met. Be kind but direct with him about what you need. Ask him how he feels about you, if there was something you did to cause him to withhold his love from you, and if there is something you can do that might make him feel warmer toward you.

"Should it be too difficult for the two of you to discuss this, ask him to accompany you to a marriage counselor or therapist. Even if he refuses, you can benefit by going yourself. You have waited long enough for him to change. Counseling should help you explore options regarding what to do about your situation."

Lack of mutual social life

Carol described her husband and herself both as loners: "We have no social life. We just don't seem to meet the right kind of people. I'm shy and it's hard for me to make friends. Do you have any suggestions?"

I gave Carol these suggestions: "To begin with, you and your husband could develop some interest or hobby together, or separately, that involves other people, whether it's tennis, bird watching, stamp collecting, folk dancing, or whatever. Also, you might consider exploring churches, classes, political and service groups, which would put you in touch with people. There are wonderful people out there. You and your husband have been alone by choice."

Lack of time together

Ann complained that her husband was always busy with his hobbies and spent hours in the garage, away from her. "I'm lonesome. I think I'd be better off single. What do you suggest?"

My response to Ann was as follows: "Let him know how lonely and dissatisfied you have been and how serious this problem is for you and your marriage. If he says he is willing to make time for you, then plan some activities that you and he can both enjoy together. I also suggest you develop some interests you can enjoy when he is busy with his hobbies. A balance of time together and time for separate interests is important for a couple. If he refuses to consider your needs at all, then you can decide what you want to do about it. Counseling or therapy can help you look at a variety of alternatives."

Power struggles

Power struggles plague many couples and lead to bitterness and frustration. Steve described his problem briefly: "My wife and I argue a lot over who's right and who's wrong. We go round and round and never resolve anything. I finally get so frustrated, I yell at her. She clams up, walks away, and doesn't talk to me for a while. We are both stubborn and neither wants to give in."

I explained the following: "There are ways of avoiding power struggles. Begin with the premise that it's okay to disagree. Because people see things differently, there are bound to be disagreements. Areas of disagreement need not turn into power struggles about who's right and who's wrong. Try to think of your own point of view as, 'This is the way I see it,' and your partner's point of view as, 'This is the way she sees it.'

"Be willing to listen and respect her point of view. Disagreements can be settled by a balance of mutual give-and-take and compromise. By a balance, I mean that you get your way some of the time, your wife gets her way some of the time, and part of the time you both compromise. (Review Chapter 1 for a detailed discussion of settling disagreements.) If you continue to have this difficulty, seek professional help.

Verbal abuse

Maria told me tearfully, "My husband has the habit of bad-mouthing me, and now my young son is beginning to do this also. My husband and I have arguments about how to discipline our 8-year-old son. I think he should be spanked when he talks back to me, but my husband doesn't agree. Something has to be done or he'll grow up bad-mouthing me like his father."

I explained my perceptions to Maria: "Children learn from their parents for better or worse, but I don't think spanking him is the answer. Corporal punishment tends to make children bitter and mean. It causes them to feel bad about themselves and about their parents. Spankings are likely to cause your son to become even angrier and more verbally abusive. I believe children should have the right to have a point of view, just like parents do. Encourage your husband and son to express their feelings and be willing to listen to their complaints. In this way they won't have to store up feelings and explode.

"Bad-mouthing and name-calling aren't necessary when people share feelings on a regular basis and have someone willing to listen without interrupting or trying to talk them out of their feelings. This does not mean that you have to give your son his way all the time or allow him to call you names. Tell him you won't allow him to call you names. But tell him he can express to you how he feels anytime he wishes (except in front of company or in public, because that would embarrass you too much)."

To those who resort to name-calling and verbal abuse, Chapter 3 should be helpful.

Physical abuse

Bruce told me his terrible temper was ruining his marriage: "I hit my wife a few times and now she has threatened to divorce me. What can I do about my temper?"

I suggested the following: "In your case, Bruce, I strongly suggest you get into therapy. Hitting your partner is very serious. In case you don't know, spouse battering is now a criminal offense. You don't have to do anything about your temper, just about what you do when you are angry. It's okay to feel angry, but not okay to hit your wife. When you feel your anger getting out of control, go for a walk to cool down. Anger and frustration can be expressed in words, not blows, name-calling, insults, or threats. I also strongly suggest you contact Batterers Anonymous."

To those who are victims of domestic violence, if you fear for your life or are being threatened, there are shelters where you can be hidden out and protected from your abuser. If you are being physically abused, call the police. The batterer will be arrested and prosecuted.

Inability to love deeply

Leonard, a man of 45, stated, "I'm married to a wonderful woman. She's everything I want in a woman. My problem is I can't feel deep love for her or anyone. I just don't seem to get emotional about anyone. I think I must be missing something important in life but I don't know what to do about it."

I explained the basic dynamics of his problem: "Not being able to feel love is a defense against being hurt and feeling pain. It's like a coat of armor some people wear to keep everyone out. But guess who's locked inside? As a child, you started out feeling a great deal, but somewhere along the way, you probably felt hurt or rejected by someone very important to you and you shut down emotionally to protect yourself from feeling pain. That numbness protected you from pain but also keeps you from feeling love and all the good things in life. Underneath all your barriers, there may be a lot of love. I suggest you get into therapy to find out. This quest might involve re-experiencing the hurt that caused you to put up your barrier in the first place."

Overdependency on parents

Sam complained, "My wife keeps running to her parents for advice instead of talking to me. This makes me furious. How can I get her to stop doing that?"

My suggestions were as follows: "Discuss this problem with her. Explain how hurt you feel and ask her to let you know what you can do to help her feel more comfortable about talking problems over with you. When she does talk to you, listen to whatever she says without interrupting her. Even encourage her to tell you more. Should you disagree with her viewpoint, respect her right to have that viewpoint. As she sees you willing to listen and doesn't find you argumentative or defensive, this will encourage her to discuss things with you again. When she does come to you with problems, after listening to her, encourage her to explore possible solutions. Ask her what she would like to see happen in that situation, rather than just giving her advice. As you become her best friend and support her growth and decision-making, she'll probably feel better about herself and about you, and she'll talk to you more often."

Dominating behavior

Avio expressed great dissatisfaction with his wife's behavior: "I'm not happy with my wife. She won't do what I want her to do. In the country where I come from, women do what their husbands say. That's how I expect my marriage to be."

To Avio, I stated the following: "In many countries, women are raised to obey their husbands and are considered their possessions. In this country, however, most women want to be treated as partners. I doubt you would want to be someone else's possession either, if given a choice.

"I suggest you either change your attitude toward your wife, or return to your land of origin and find a woman who is willing to obey you. I must tell you that the kind of relationship you are seeking tends to breed hostility rather than love. You are likely to get far more satisfaction and love from a woman if you treat her more as an equal and less like a servant or a child."

To those whose partner is domineering and those who are feeling oppressed, I suggest counseling or therapy. If your partner is not willing to participate, individual therapy can help you to grow and to evaluate your options.

Alcoholism

Carmen was crying as she described her husband's weekend behavior: "My husband is a weekend alcoholic. He is a good father and husband during the week, but on the weekend, he drinks, gets mean, and begins hitting me in front of the children. Afterward, he doesn't even remember doing it. He denies he has a drinking problem. I've threatened to leave him if he won't go for help because I can't stand it anymore. But he refuses to go. What should I do?"

I suggested the following: "Excellent help is available for partners and families of persons with drinking problems through Al-Anon, part of Alcoholics Anonymous. Al-Anon is designed to help family members deal with the person who has a drinking problem in a constructive, helpful way.

"Aside from it being dangerous for you to be hit, it is extremely damaging for your children to be exposed to these acts of physical violence. At least for their sakes, you really must do something to stop this, even if it means calling the police and having your husband arrested. If he wakes up in jail, maybe he'll realize he has a problem."

To the alcohol abuser: You are probably in denial regarding your drinking problem. If your partner is complaining about your drinking, I urge you to contact Alcoholics Anonymous to find out the truth about your drinking before it's too late.

Trying to change a partner

Adrienne explained that during the 35 years she and her husband have been married her husband let her control everything.

She added, "Now that I want him to take more responsibility and make some decisions, he refuses. He is treating me like a total stranger, and I feel so hurt. I don't know what to do."

I gave Adrienne my perceptions: "Trying to change a partner is a no-win situation that leads to frustration and resistance. People can change if they feel motivated to do so, but most people resist when being pushed.

"It sounds to me like you are changing and, in turn, are trying to change your husband. When one partner in a relationship changes, the whole relationship is thrown off balance for a while. You might be coming down too hard on your husband with your new demands. He probably feels threatened. Rather than demanding sudden, radical changes in him, gently and subtly encourage him to make some decisions, even minor ones at first. Gradually take a less assertive role in decision-making yourself and involve him more and more by asking him what he thinks or what he would like to do in certain situations. When he does help in decision-making, praise and support him for those decisions he does make. Gradually he may come to feel more confident and more willing to take on more responsibilities. Don't expect major changes or shifts in behavior overnight. Have a little patience. Changes in behavior take time. Your own has taken 35 years."

Unwillingness to share work

Donna related, "I'm having a problem. All my husband wants to do when he comes home from work is watch TV. He thinks because he has worked all day, he's entitled to sit around and relax. But when I come home from work, he expects me to do everything, because he thinks the housework and kids are woman's work. His dad didn't help his mom, either. I'm tired of doing everything myself. How can I get him to help me?"

I suggested the following: "You have the right to expect help, especially when you are a working mother. I would approach him in a loving, rather than hostile or threatening, way. Ask him to suggest a time when you and he could talk. When that time arrives, explain that you need his help to find a solution. Then let him know that you are not willing to do all the work yourself and you need his help with housework and the children. Give him a chance to choose which household chores he would be willing to take responsibility for on a regular basis. Also, ask if he would be willing to spend some time each evening with the children, playing, reading to them, helping them with their homework, bathing them, and putting them to bed. Let him know that, with his help, you will likely be less tired and more fun. Also thank him whenever he does help. Your positive attitude will help him feel better about helping.

"In case he refuses, you might wish to discuss the possibility of quitting your job and staying home to do all the work, or hiring someone to clean for you. If you and he can't work this out yourselves, seek professional help."

Wanting another chance

Amy told me that her husband and she were separated. She added remorsefully, "I realize I ran all over him, but he didn't say anything. He'd take it and take it until he'd finally explode. I'd apologize, but he never seemed satisfied. He's keeping a grudge against me and says he doesn't want to see me again. I know things could be different now, if he'd only give me another chance."

I explained to Amy that, if her husband wouldn't see her, there was nothing she could do. I also made these suggestions: "Amy, you might try writing to him and asking if he would be willing to go with you to a marriage counselor. Tell him you now realize that you were domineering and took advantage of him, and you are willing to learn to change your ways of relating to him. If he refuses to go with you or to answer your letter, I suggest you go for therapy yourself, which will give you support through this crisis and help you grow and learn from your experiences.

Suspiciousness and jealousy

Didi cried as she described her problem: "I've been married for five years and I feel like a prisoner. My husband is very jealous.

He wants to know where I am every minute. When someone calls me, he wants to know who it is. I've never given him any reason to be worried or suspicious about me. When I go shopping and come home a few minutes late, he gets upset and asks where I've been. I'm tired of being questioned. One of these days, I'll leave him if he doesn't stop this stuff."

I gave Didi my perception of the situation: "Sounds like your husband is afraid of losing you. If you haven't given him any reason to feel insecure or suspicious, perhaps he may have doubts about his own self-worth and ability to hold your love. I suggest you give him lots of love, affection, attention, and reassurance. Be sure to tell him that his behavior could drive you away because it is both stifling and humiliating for you.

"It would be wise, in this case, to insist he see a therapist. Very insecure people do actually drive their loved ones away without even realizing that they themselves have caused it. As far as your feeling like a prisoner, it is up to you to decide how much independence and freedom you want and need, and how much you are willing to restrict yourself to please your husband."

Pressure to stay married

Henry explained that his wife had pressured him into getting married in the first place and was now pressuring him not to get a divorce: "I left her several times and she came chasing after me. I'm back with her now and I don't know what to do."

I told Henry, "You say your wife pressured you into getting married and into staying with her. Please understand that you are allowing yourself to be pressured into it. Even if your wife were very forceful, you could still leave if you wanted to. Part of you may want to stay. I suggest you see a therapist to find answers to these questions: Why aren't you willing to take charge of your own life? What direction do you really want to take? Going back and forth is just hurting your wife and yourself without resolving your problem."

Feeling left out after birth of a baby

Bob and his wife had just had a baby boy two weeks ago. He described his problem: "I helped with the birth and was looking forward to helping my wife care for our son. Instead, her parents came to stay with us and they're doing everything. I feel left out. I don't want to say anything to my wife or her parents about what I'm feeling because that might upset them, so I just keep my feelings to myself and I leave the house when I'm upset. How can I handle this delicately?"

I suggested the following: "You might begin by telling your wife how you feel. Otherwise, a distance will develop between the two of you. You and your wife should discuss ways of handling the situation. Many new fathers feel left out unless they participate actively in caring for their baby. The first few weeks are a very important time for you and your wife and son to be together. You or she might decide to explain this to her parents. If so, you might tell them that this is a very special time for you and you want to help care for your baby when you are at home. When you are not home, they can help your wife care for the baby. Tell them all this in a nice way and thank them for all their help."

Prenuptial agreements

Eve had been married 10 years. This was her husband's second marriage. She stated her problem: "I have never felt good about our marriage, because before we were married, my husband insisted I sign a prenuptial agreement saying I am not entitled to any of his property, except for half interest in our family home. I was desperate to marry him, so I signed it. Our relationship seems to be getting worse and I'm thinking of getting a divorce. Don't you think it was unfair of him to ask me to sign that agreement?"

I gave Eve my perspective: "I don't see it as necessarily a question of fairness and I don't know his circumstances. Sometimes when people were married before and have assets and children from their former marriage, they want to see that the property they owned prior to their second marriage will go to their children. I don't see this as unfair. It has to do with trying to protect one's children.

"I would like to see you taking some responsibility for what has happened. You signed the agreement and didn't take a stand at that time. Now, you can choose to accept it as something that happened 10 years ago and get on with your relationship, or, if you just can't live with it, decide what you want to do about it. The worst thing for you is keeping this resentment going. It is robbing you of all the good things in life that you could have now and is costing you more than you can imagine."

Financial problems

Sandra was deeply troubled. She explained, "My husband and I have been married three years. We live in the home I owned before we got married. I had it all paid for and I had to work only two days a week to keep it up. I was in good shape. Then I met my husband. Our relationship was perfect. I put him on a pedestal. After we got married, he began to complain about not having any security himself and he asked me to work full-time. I did this to please him, but I resented it. I bought a car for him, which he considers his own, and we are struggling to pay the bills he runs up.

"He complains a lot about money and says he can't afford to take me out for dinner. The tension builds between us and then we argue. I'm so angry, I feel like hitting him. At this point, I love him but I don't trust him. This is my third marriage. I came away from the other two without anything. I'm never going to give him any part of my house."

My suggestions were the following: "You're very angry with him for making your financial situation worse than it was, and you're worried that he's out to take what's yours. To protect yourself, you can make out a will leaving your house to whomever you choose. Check with an attorney on this matter.

"Regarding your work schedule: If working full-time is making you feel angry and resentful, consider going back to part-time work and adjusting your expenditures to your combined income. If your husband wants more money, then he can look for a higher-paying job.

"Your resentments are eroding away what is left of your relationship. I suggest you and he work out a budget you can both agree on and set limits on spending. You may wish to consult a financial advisor to help you. With a limited budget, if your husband is a fortune-seeker, as you seem to suspect, he will probably move on. Otherwise, hopefully, the two of you can make a life together based on what you and he can afford."

Possessiveness

Kevin and his wife were married seven years when he left. He explained his reasons for leaving: "Kay was like a little kid hanging onto me. I worked five days a week and she was okay with that, but she wanted me to spend every minute of my free time with her. She wouldn't even let me see my family. I just couldn't take it anymore and I'm not going back to her. I'd die if I stayed in that relationship."

My perceptions were the following: "From what you say, it sounds like Kay was very insecure and needy and you were feeling smothered. Possessive individuals rarely realize that their behavior pushes loved ones away. They are often insatiable. It is very important for Kay to work with a therapist who could help her grow up. You might consider going for counseling together, especially if there are children involved."

Loneliness

Don explained, "I've had feelings of loneliness ever since I can remember. I have a great family and a wonderful wife, and yet, no matter where I am or who's around, I feel lonely. What can I do?"

I gave Don my perceptions: "The word 'lonely' connotes being separate or alone. I suspect your feelings of loneliness started very early, perhaps even in infancy. I strongly suggest you find a therapist to help you explore its roots and work those feelings through. The Process for Reducing Ingrained Tension and Anxiety (see Chapter 4) could also be very beneficial for you."

Lack of commitment

Joan had been living with Tony for more than two years and had hoped to marry him. With tears in her eyes, she related, "He's saying he's not sure he wants to get married. I'm 39 already and I want children. I can't wait for him forever. It all seems so hopeless. I don't understand why he's holding back. We get along great and he knows I love him. I should leave him now because there's really no point in my living with him any longer."

I gave her my perception: "Committing oneself to one special person can be very scary for some people, especially if they have been hurt or rejected by someone they loved. Other factors involved are finding the 'right' person and timing. Perhaps you are the 'right' person, but he's not ready; or he might be ready, but you are not the 'right' person. It would be important for you to find out his true feelings either way. You might ask him to go with you to a marriage counselor to discuss this, in case he's having a problem sorting out his feelings.

"Better to find out his true feelings and concerns now than later. If his feelings are ambivalent and he can't seem to work through them, you would be wise not to marry him even if he were to ask you. The reason for this is that the likelihood of your marriage lasting would be slim. A partner who does not feel positive and committed is no prize. Your love for him is not enough."

Wanting to be single

Evan and his wife were both 23 years old. They had been married for a little more than one year, and Evan wanted to leave. He stated, "I don't like being married. I just want to be single again. We've known each other for a long time. We used to be best friends. I never dated other girls, but now I'm interested in other women. I'm very unhappy and I seem to have lost my passion for my wife. I know it's wrong, but I've been seeing some other women lately. I finally told my wife, hoping that she'd tell me to leave, but instead she said we could work it out. She's overly dependent on me and that makes me feel terrible. I don't want to hurt her, but I don't want to be married to her, either. When I tell her I'm going to leave, after we talk, I tell her I'll stay. What do you think I should do?"

My response was as follows: "Evan, you and your wife are both very young. I cannot tell you whether to stay or leave, but what I do suggest is that you and your wife see a marriage counselor. This could help you in several ways: First of all, it can give both of you a chance to look at your relationship and how each of you are responsible for what is happening now. It can help you look at the alternatives you have and can give your wife support, should you decide to leave her. Also, counseling can give you both a deeper understanding of your own feelings, needs, and behavior, and assist you in making choices about your marriage and your life. Afterward, if you can't rescue your marriage, at least you will know you tried. Otherwise, years from now, you may have deep regrets that you didn't even try."

Feeling like a victim

Sadly, Indira stated, "My husband and I and our two sons came to the United States about two years ago. Then I began to see that I was being treated like a slave, not a wife. I work and my husband goes to college. He's never home. When he comes home, he dresses up and goes out wherever he pleases, leaving me at home with the children to do all the work. I'm very angry and frustrated with him. It's not fair. When I complain, he laughs and says I'm crazy. I have wanted to leave him for a long time, but I'm afraid of being alone. If I leave him, he won't help me with the children. After working so hard for so many years to support him, I will end up with nothing. He says he owes me nothing. He thinks he's a king and he can do anything he wants. What can I do?"

I told her the following: "You don't have to be a slave unless you choose to be treated like one. Fortunately, in the United States women enjoy a more equal status with men. This may be difficult for your husband to accept, especially if you come from a country where women are considered second-class citizens and property of their husbands.

"Marriage counseling might be very helpful for both of you and give you emotional support through that transition. In case you decide to leave him, you could probably manage, because you have been supporting him and your family anyhow and you sound far from being a helpless person. Once your husband begins working, a lawyer could advise you regarding obtaining child support from him for your sons.

"As far as you being afraid of being alone, you are pretty much alone anyway. I encourage you not to see yourself as the victim. Instead, begin taking responsibility for creating a satisfying life for yourself and your sons, either with or without him."

When romance is gone

John told me sadly, "I've been married seven years and all the romance seems to be gone. All that's left is a feeling of responsibility for things that have to be done. That's how my parents' marriage was. I'm not sure I even love my wife or ever did. I was very young when we got married. I always wanted to be married and I feel very safe with her, but now I'm thinking about leaving. I don't want to hurt my kids. What do you think I should do?"

I gave John my perception: "Staying or leaving is a decision you will have to make. Because you are confused, I suggest you seek the help of a therapist before making a decision. It sounds like you needed this kind of help before you got married. When people, such as yourself, marry just to be married, without love or deep caring for the other person, it rarely leads to satisfaction and romance. Such marriages usually end up becoming marriages of convenience, instead of love affairs. Feeling safe is usually not enough to satisfy people.

"It would be wise and beneficial for you and your wife to get some marriage counseling as soon as possible. Perhaps you can still find love and satisfaction together. If not, you can discuss a separation, how to prepare the children, and how to work together as parents after the separation."

Criticism

Ted described his dilemma: "My wife often asks me to critique her artwork. When I do, in a constructive way, she becomes offended and complains that I don't like anything she makes. I do like most of what she makes and I try to be as constructive as possible in my criticism. Should I refuse to comment when she asks me to and avoid these disturbing arguments and accusations?"

I explained to Ted that nobody likes criticism, and some people take criticism harder than others, especially when it comes to creative work: "Chances are she's looking for your support and approval more than your criticism. It might help, before making any suggestions, to begin by telling her what you do like about her work. If you do make suggestions, discuss what you believe could be changed, added, or deleted to make it even better. Don't argue with her if she doesn't accept your suggestions. It's not worth it. Generally speaking, criticism can be deadly to a relationship. Your relationship is more important than arguing over her artwork. Her work will either be accepted by others, or it won't. It will probably be easier for her to accept negative feedback from others than from you, so I suggest you keep any criticism to a minimum.

"I realize you are in a most difficult position because your wife is asking you to critique her work. This puts you on the spot. It sounds, though, that she really wants and needs your approval and encouragement. There are two appropriate old sayings for your dilemma: 'If you can't say anything nice, don't say anything' and 'You can attract more bees with honey than you can with vinegar.'"

Step-children

Jill married a man with two daughters, ages 11 and 13, from his first marriage. She stated, "I'm ready to divorce him because his mother and his first wife keep pushing him to see his kids. I used to have his kids over, but not anymore. I want a child of my own, and he made me get an abortion. He says he doesn't want any more children. I won't baby-sit his kids if he doesn't want my child."

I gave Jill my perception: "I see two issues here that you seem to be lumping together. Each issue should be considered separately. One issue is your wanting a child. You blame him for the abortion. You could have chosen not to have it. You are angry with him for not wanting 'your' child. I suggest you discuss this with him or see a counselor together. Find out what his concerns are about having another child. If you cannot reach an agreement, then you must decide what you want to do about it. Your decision should be based on how much it means to you to have a child and whether you are prepared to give up this marriage over this issue.

"Regarding the issue of your husband seeing his children from his first marriage: I encourage you not to take your anger and frustration for your husband out on his children. His children need to see their father, and he has a responsibility to see them. It is extremely important that you cooperate about this. Turning your back on his children only complicates and worsens your situation. Not only will it cause big problems for him and his children, but will damage the relationship between you and your husband, and make it less likely for him to want a baby with you. These are very complex issues you are dealing with and I suggest you and your husband seek some professional help."

In-laws

Alberto and his wife have been married for almost five years. He stated his problem: "My wife is from a large family, and ever since we got married, we have had members of her family living with us. Now, my wife is very angry with me because I asked her sister and brother-in-law and their three children to leave after being with us for five months. We have been very crowded with five extra people in our two-bedroom apartment. I want to be alone with my wife and baby for once. Is that too much to ask?"

I gave Alberto my perspective: "I suggest you and she discuss this matter and set up some ground rules for house guests and relatives. House guests are fun to have when they come for a few days—or a few weeks, maximum—but when they stay on and on, it wears on a couple and makes it difficult to have time alone together. Explain to your wife that you need time alone with her and your child. Tell her you are willing to have house guests for short periods of time, but not for more than two or three weeks at a time. Marriage counseling might be helpful if you and she can't reach an agreement on this issue."

Crisis of losing parents

Gigi told me she was thinking of leaving her husband: "I've been really depressed for about two years since my mother died. At first, my husband was understanding, but after a few weeks as my depression continued, he just started getting more involved in sports and hobbies. Now, we're just like strangers. Even my health is going downhill. I feel very alone."

I explained: "When a person is feeling depressed, things usually seem hopeless. I want you to know that help is available. The death of a parent can lead to a crisis in some people. It is normal to mourn the loss of a loved one, but if the period of mourning drags on the way yours has, it's really important to seek help. I suggest you go to a medical doctor about your health and a psychiatrist about your depression. I also advise you and your husband to seek a marriage counselor about your marriage. You've let this go too long. Believe it or not, you can still put some joy and meaning back into your life. Your mother would have wanted that for you."

To the partner of a grieving person, I encourage patience, empathy, and lots of love and affection. This too shall pass.

Separation

Roanne commented that she didn't know where to go or what to do: "My husband says he plans to leave me. He doesn't talk to me or give me any money. I don't even know why. He just does what he wants and doesn't tell me anything. We have a beautiful little daughter, 1 year old. He loves her a lot and spends a lot of time with her. I have no family here, and I still love my husband. I can't accept a separation. What can I do to save my marriage?"

My response to Roanne was the following: "There may not be anything you can do to save your marriage. If your husband is determined to leave you, you can't make him stay. You might ask him if he would go with you to see a marriage counselor, and if he won't agree to counseling, then I suggest you go yourself. Because you are feeling so helpless and alone, counseling can give you support and confidence to learn how to handle the emotional, social, and financial problems that face couples when they separate.

"In order to prevent future problems for your daughter, I suggest you avoid emotional scenes in front of her. Your daughter needs two parents. Even if you two should divorce, I urge you to cooperate with her father about raising her. Should the separation continue, you may need to contact a Family Law attorney to help you work out details regarding your daughter and financial arrangements."

Divorce

Alex said he made a terrible mistake about one year ago: "My wife said she wanted a divorce and went to an attorney. He drew up all the divorce papers, but she kept putting off signing them. One day I went to her attorney's office with her. She still wouldn't sign the papers, so I decided to do her a favor and sign them for her. Well, from that time on, she has not spoken to me. I feel terrible that I signed those divorce papers. Maybe if I hadn't, we would still be together. She's the only woman I have ever loved. I want other people to know about this so they won't make the same mistake I did."

My response to Alex was as follows: "It's possible she hesitated signing the divorce papers because she really didn't want the divorce, or she might have wanted the divorce but felt too insecure. It's hard to know what was going on with her then or what would have happened had you not signed the divorce papers. But what seems to be going on with you is that you're beating yourself over the head for signing the papers and blaming yourself for the divorce.

"If you haven't told her already that you love her and the reason you signed the divorce papers, then you might wish to write to her and let her know this. Also, ask her to write back or call you. If she doesn't respond or won't talk with you, then you will have done everything you can. In time, hopefully, you will come to accept the divorce and get on with your life."

Depression and suicidal tendencies

Patti confided that she has been feeling very depressed for a few months and has been thinking about taking her life. She explained her reasons: "I'm married to a wonderful man, but for a long time now, he's had a dream of moving away from the city, far into the country. A few months ago he told me he is planning to quit his job soon and said he then wants to move away. I don't want to leave my home, my grown children, and my family, but I can't tell him that. It would spoil his dream. It's been very hard for me to hide my feelings from him. I just hate to hurt him or spoil things for him."

My response to Patti was the following: "You will be hurting your husband a lot less if you tell him how you feel. If you were to kill yourself, that will surely spoil his dream. I suggest you level with him about how depressed you have been feeling about moving away and about your committing suicide. Tell him how much you have tried to hide this from him, so as not to spoil his dream, how much you want to please him, and how impossible this all seems to you. Afterward, listen to what he has to say and discuss this with him.

"This is a matter of life and death. If you are not honest with him about your feelings, he will be terribly hurt, and you will be dead. Think how unfair that would be to your husband, not even giving him the chance to discuss this with you and to work out something that could be a satisfactory solution for both of you.

"I also strongly urge you to set an appointment immediately with a psychiatrist to discuss your depression. Perhaps you need an antidepression medicine to get you through this period."

Disciplining the children

Nori and her husband argued a lot about how to discipline their 2½-year-old son, Adam. Nori explained, "When we got married, I didn't want any children. When I got pregnant accidentally, I was very upset about it, but I didn't want to get an abortion. After the baby came, I looked to my husband for a lot of help in raising our son. Instead, I have to do most of the disciplining myself. When Adam doesn't listen, I take a little stick and switch his legs; or when Adam won't eat what I fix, I let him go hungry. That makes my husband upset and we argue over it. I'm losing respect for my husband. I thought he'd be a strong father, and instead he's weak."

My reply may not have been what Nori was expecting: "I don't know how you were brought up, but thinking about your taking a little stick and switching a 2½-year-old's legs is very upsetting. In the United States, hitting children with sticks and withholding meals are considered child abuse and child neglect. Psychologically, using harsh punishments is destructive to children and makes them mean and hostile, or breaks their spirit.

"I urge you to seek professional help and parenting advice. What Adam needs from you is a lot of love, affection, and praise when he does cooperate. He will want to listen to you more. Realistic limits should be set for his behavior and appropriate discipline be given. There are fine books on parenting and on disciplining children available in libraries.

"About his not wanting to eat what you have fixed, I suggest you offer him an alternative food that is easily available, such as fruit, milk, bread with peanut butter and jam, or cheese. It doesn't pay to have power struggles about food. Avoid power struggles with your son as much as possible. Giving in on little things and standing firm on important issues was the principle I followed in raising my three children. Two years old is the age for temper tantrums. If he throws a tantrum about not getting his way, let him kick and scream if he wants to, but don't punish him for having the tantrum. He will calm down after a while. You might also try distracting him with a toy or game or taking him out for a walk.

"About your husband not being strong, I see it as a sign of strength to handle children with gentleness, kindness, firmness, and patience. The result can be warm, loving children."

Homosexuality

Gina was devastated when she found out that her husband was gay: "We have been married for six years and we have a 3-year-old daughter. For all this time I didn't know that he had a male lover. But I began to get suspicious because he was gone so much, and I had him followed. He hasn't told anyone about this and he doesn't want his parents to know.

"I am very confused now about what to do. He refuses to give up his lover. Aside from this problem, he has been a wonderful husband and father. He says he wants to stay married to me, but I don't know whether I can live with him, knowing that he goes off to his lover while I sit at home alone, feeling rejected and inadequate as a woman. I'm not the kind of woman to go out looking for another man while I'm still married. I would like to stay married but I'm feeling upset all the time and worried I might get AIDS. What do you think would be the best thing to do?"

I gave Gina my perspective: "Too bad he didn't have the courage to tell you he was gay before he married you. He was probably afraid you wouldn't marry him if you knew. It must have been a terrible shock, finding out the way you did. Apparently he did a good job of hiding it.

"You say you feel rejected and inadequate as a woman. Even if you were the most desirable woman in the world, if your husband is homosexual, he would still prefer a male lover. Don't be hard on yourself. Try to understand that your husband cannot help his sexual preference. His mistake was not having told you about it.

"As far as what to do now, that is a decision you must make for yourself. Because you are confused as to what to do, I would suggest you seek professional help before making any decision. Therapy can help you work through your anger and disappointment and help you look at various options. Because you are concerned about AIDS, insist that your husband take an AIDS test, and if you and he are sexually active, be sure to practice safe sex."

Sexual impotence

Darla confided that her husband has been sexually impotent for several years: "He feels very bad about it and I end up feeling very frustrated. Aside from this problem, we have a very good marriage. Is there anything that can be done for this problem?"

I responded: "There certainly is. Impotence in men can be reversed in most cases. It is highly advisable to have a medical evaluation done first to find out if his impotence is from physical causes. If there is no physical basis for it, then find a therapist who specializes in sexual problems. Some university medical schools have human sexuality clinics. Men are extremely sensitive about this type of problem, and once they begin to worry about not being able to get an erection, it is even more difficult for them to achieve one. It is best if you can put him at ease and be patient, loving, and affectionate. Avoid putting him down for having this problem or talking about this to family or friends. Impotence is involuntary, not something he can help."

"Open" marriage

Jay's wife was leaving him for another man. Jay explained. "I still can't believe it is over for us. I thought we had a good marriage. About six months ago, I asked her if she would mind switching partners with a couple we were friendly with. When she said no, I dropped it. Afterward, I noticed she seemed distant, and six months later she began having an affair with the man she is now living with. I'm hoping she'll come back to me. I made a commitment to her for life. I'll never give her up. What can I do to get her back?"

My response to Jay was the following: "Your wife probably felt very hurt about your suggestion to switch partners. This may have caused her to feel unloved and unable to satisfy you sexually. That hurt might well have resulted in her turning away from you and seeking someone else. The commitment you say you made for life ended when you suggested switching partners. Of the couples I have counseled with open marriages, in each case, one of the partners told me that his or her feelings of anger, rejection, insecurity, and guilt caused a weakening of and eventual an end to their relationship.

Mental illness

Ed recently left his wife. He described his reason: "My wife is mentally ill and is getting worse. She refuses to continue seeing her psychiatrist and is becoming so hostile, abusive, and suspicious with me that I had to get out of that situation. I intend to continue supporting her financially, but I still feel ashamed for leaving her."

My response to Ed was as follows: "Double binds are very difficult, especially when they involve loved ones. When you left, you felt guilty, and if you had stayed, you might have gone down the tubes with your wife. At least this way, you can help her. It sounds like she might need immediate psychiatric intervention. I suggest you contact the mental health department in your area. In case it becomes necessary, a psychiatric emergency team (PET) could go to her home. If her condition is severe enough, they might find it necessary to hospitalize her temporarily and evaluate what kind of care and treatment would be most beneficial for her."

When sexual appetites vary

Sexual appetites vary from person to person, just like appetites for food. Sexual problems can result when differences are too great. Gregg described his situation: "Joanne and I have a close, loving relationship, but we struggle with one problem. I am a sexy guy with a strong sexual appetite; Joanne enjoys sex occasionally. She's rarely interested or in the mood. For years I have been reluctant to complain because I didn't want to rock the boat. There were times when I was tempted to seek out another sexual partner, but I didn't want to be unfaithful to Joanne. I have often felt depressed and rejected, but I kept my feelings to myself. Lately, I'm beginning to resent my situation more and more, and I'm considering separating."

I suggested the following: "Not working on this problem together puts your relationship at great risk and leaves both of you feeling unloved and lonely. Gregg, you have waited too long and suffered too much. You must tell Joanne what is going on with you and strongly urge her to go with you to a licensed therapist who specializes in sexual therapy. If she refuses to go, seek counseling for yourself."

Unfaithfulness

Unfaithfulness is a complex problem that causes great unhappiness for many couples. Ann telephoned and asked to see me alone. She explained, "I'm not usually a jealous person, but I'm insanely jealous of a very attractive woman my husband works with. Sometimes he drives her to and from work. I know he's interested in her. I'm afraid he's going to get involved with this woman sexually. He and I have had an agreement to be faithful to each other, but he has broken our agreement twice. He confessed he was unfaithful at two stag parties when he was drunk. He promised never to do it again. I would like to believe him but I'm not sure I can. I know we love each other and I don't want to blow this out of proportion. I don't want to lose him. How should I handle this?"

I gave her my perspective: "You can't keep your husband faithful. Remaining faithful to one's partner is a decision each person makes on his or her own. Also, nothing can be done now about your husband's past transgressions. What you can do now is decide what you want to do from now on. Because faithfulness is an important value for you, you must decide whether you are willing to accept more unfaithfulness in the future. If not, then tell your husband your decision and let him know about your concerns regarding his female co-worker."

"If you feel strongly about leaving him should he ever be unfaithful to you again, tell him this and what you are prepared to do. When your husband senses your strength and determination and knows you mean business, then he will have the choice of remaining faithful to you or losing you, and he will do what he will do. You can't control him. Worrying won't help him remain faithful to you. After telling him how you feel about this situation, I suggest you not bug him about it or bring up his past transgressions. Instead, use your energy for developing a close, caring, affectionate, loving, fun, and sexually exciting relationship with him. This might lessen your chances of his being unfaithful to you in the future."

To those partners or spouses who are in committed relationships, I wish to say that I believe sex should be exclusively with your partner. I speak from the point of view of both a pragmatist and a counselor. If you cheat on your partner and think it won't matter, or that it won't hurt anyone, you are mistaken. Not only will it hurt you and your partner, but also the third party and any children involved. And if your partner did not find out, you would still suffer because you would know about your indiscretion; this will affect your relationship adversely.

A sexual encounter with someone other than your partner will ultimately cause a rift or breach in the relationship with your partner, a weakening of the bonds, which will slowly erode the closeness you once had. You would also have to live with feeling worse about yourself, and therefore have less love to give your loved ones. In case this isn't reason enough for staying faithful, consider the major physical risk of AIDS and venereal disease.

Temptation is everywhere. The big question you have to ask yourself is: "Is this affair really worth losing everything?" Decisions you make affect the rest of your life. If you are in a committed relationship, and feel you must have an affair with a third party, I strongly believe the most honorable thing to do is separate from your partner beforehand. A much less traumatic alternative of course would be to work with your own partner on improving your own sexual relationship.

Even in the best of relationships, there are bound to be problems. As I mentioned in the introduction to this chapter, the perspective and suggestions I offered for each problem are not cure-alls, and many of my responses should be considered merely as a first step toward improving a difficult situation, many of which may require professional help to resolve. When physical abuse is involved, I urge the abused partner to save himself or herself and any children involved and seek professional help. Referral resources can be found in Chapter 8.

Leaving problems unresolved brings with it great risk to the physical and emotional well-being of both partners. The longer a problem persists, the more strain is placed on the relationship and the greater likelihood for a couple of splitting up. I therefore urge couples to take their problems seriously and resolve them as soon as they can, either on their own or with the help of a professional therapist.

CHAPTER 7

Healing Troubled Relationships

Grudges, misgivings, and regrets keep many of us stuck in the past, and give us little rest, peace, or happiness. Forgiveness is a great healer. This involves forgiving ourselves, forgiving others, and seeking forgiveness from others. We can't go back and repeat the past, and tormenting ourselves does us and our loved ones great harm. Only by learning, growing from our own experiences, and in forgiving ourselves and others can we find peace and happiness.

Three Forgiveness Processes

The three forgiveness processes that follow are designed to help you achieve inner peace. The first brings about a state of self-forgiveness through re-experiencing the past and helping us see ourselves as growing individuals who learn from our experiences. The second process helps us forgive others through communicating past resentments and regrets. The third helps us ask for forgiveness from others.

Forgiving yourself

Before beginning this process, make a list of situations for which you have not forgiven yourself. Set aside 10 to 15 minutes to work on each situation.

Step 1. Focus on one situation at a time, visualizing yourself in that particular situation. Mentally review the details of what happened.

Step 2. What role or part did you have in causing that situation to turn out the way it did then?

Step 3. What regrets do you have now for the way you handled that situation?

Step 4. Knowing what you know now, what would you have done differently?

Step 5. What have you learned from that experience?

Step 6. See yourself as a growing person who learns from past experiences, has self-compassion, and forgives past mistakes and shortcomings. Then forgive yourself and allow yourself to experience a release.

Step 7. Repeat steps 1 through 6 for each different situation.

Forgiving others

Forgiving another person does not mean we condone that person's behavior or the way we were treated. Forgiveness serves to release us from the negativity and pain of not forgiving and brings us peace.

This process provides a simple, yet powerful way of helping you forgive others, including those from whom you may be estranged or who are deceased. It can be done silently, aloud, or in writing. This process is my adaptation of a forgiveness process developed by Dr. Harold Bloomfield, described in his book, *Making Peace With Your Parents*. The example below demonstrates how one woman used this forgiveness process for forgiving her deceased father:

"I want to forgive you, Dad, but you were terrible when I was growing up. I want to forgive you, Dad, but you were never there when I needed you. I want to forgive you, Dad, but you were always critical of me. I want to forgive you, Dad, but you called me names and put me down. I want to forgive you, Dad, but you were very selfish and had to have everything your way. I want to forgive you, Dad, but you isolated yourself from our family. I want to forgive you, Dad, but you had a terrible temper and I was afraid of you. I want to forgive you, Dad, but you were so mean and rigid. I want to forgive you, Dad, but I needed love and affection from you, and you pushed me away. I want to forgive you, Dad, but you hurt me by doing that. I want to forgive you, Dad, but I wanted you to love me and be gentle with me. I want to forgive you, Dad, but you were so angry all the time. I want to forgive you, Dad, but you treated us like crap. I want to forgive you, Dad, but everything had to be your way. I want to forgive you, Dad, but why couldn't you have given in to me once in a while? I want to forgive you, Dad, but you made me feel afraid and insecure. I want to forgive you, Dad, but I felt lonely and unloved by you. I want to forgive you, Dad, but I needed your love desperately. I want to forgive you, Dad; I loved you but I could never tell you I did. I want to forgive you, Dad, but there were times that when I was little I wished you were dead. I want to forgive you, Dad, but if only I could have told you how angry I was I would have forgiven you then. I want to forgive you, Dad, but you never let me tell you how I felt. I want to forgive you, Dad, but you were so hard on all of us. I want to forgive you, Dad, but you kept us from loving you. I want to forgive you, Dad, but you made my life miserable. I want to forgive you, Dad, but you never told me you loved me. I want to forgive you, Dad, but I needed to hear that from you. I want to forgive you, Dad, but you were so strict with me. I want to forgive you, Dad, but I needed to hear, 'I love you.' I want to forgive you, Dad, but you never said it. I want to forgive you, Dad, but you held back your love from me. I want to forgive you, Dad, but you held back love from everyone. I want to forgive you, Dad, but you lived a very lonely life. I want to forgive you, Dad, but you closed yourself in a shell. I want to forgive you, Dad, but you wouldn't let me in. I want to forgive you, Dad, but you were a very unhappy person. I want to forgive you, Dad, but you wasted your life being angry. I want to forgive you, Dad, but I missed your love. I want to forgive you, Dad, but you missed out. I want to forgive you, Dad, but we both missed out. I want to forgive you, Dad, but I feel sad. I want to forgive you, Dad, but I wish it could have been different. I want to forgive you, Dad, but...I want to forgive you, Dad, but..., I do forgive you Dad."

Instructions for forgiving others

Step 1. Focus on a person you have not yet forgiven and say or write, "I want to forgive you (name of the person), but..." Complete the sentence by adding a reason why you can't forgive that person. For example: "I want to forgive you, Dad, but you treated me so unfairly."

Step 2. Repeat Step 1, "I want to forgive you (name the person), but...." Again, complete the sentence by adding another reason why you can't forgive that person. For example: "I want to forgive you, Dad, but you were too harsh with me."

Step 3. Repeat, "I want to forgive you (name the person), but...." Again, complete the sentence.

Step 4. Repeat this format over and over again, each time completing the sentence by adding a different reason why you can't forgive that person. There is no limit to how many times you can do this. Continue until you can't think of any more reasons not to forgive that person, and the words come out simply, "I want to forgive you. I want to forgive you. I do forgive you." Then experience the release that comes with forgiving that person. Remember that carrying anger and resentments from the past hurts only you, and by forgiving, you are likely to feel freer and more at peace.

Seeking forgiveness from others

After forgiving yourself and forgiving others, a final touch is seeking forgiveness *from* others. This process can be said silently, aloud, or in writing, and is especially helpful when direct communication cannot take place. Please note that seeking forgiveness from others for something you have done only has meaning if the action you seek forgiveness for is not repeated. Some individuals repeatedly beg for forgiveness for committing abusive acts and continue that abusive behavior. Such people need counseling or therapy to gain insight and control over their problems. Before beginning this process, make a list of those from whom you are seeking forgiveness.

The example that follows demonstrates this process being used by a woman seeking forgiveness from her mother who died 20 years ago.

"Please forgive me, Mom; I neglected you and I didn't look out for you the way I should have. Please forgive me,

Mom; I didn't realize how sick you were. Please forgive me, Mom; I realized after it was too late. Please forgive me, Mom; I feel I am to blame for your suffering toward the end. Please forgive me, Mom; I should have moved you to a better facility after the first owner left. Please forgive me, Mom; I just left you there after the care deteriorated. Please forgive me, Mom; I should have looked for a better place for you. Please forgive me, Mom; I should have checked to find out what was wrong with you sooner. Please forgive me, Mom; I called the doctor too late. Please forgive me, Mom; I couldn't stand to see you suffering the way you did. Please forgive me, Mom; I was relieved when you died. Please forgive me, Mom; I didn't want you to suffer so much. Please forgive me, Mom; I still have visions of you writhing in pain and moaning. Please forgive me, Mom; I wish I could have helped you and spared you all that pain. Please forgive me, Mom; I had little babies to care for then and I couldn't spend much time with you. Please forgive me, Mom; I need your forgiveness. Please forgive me, Mom; I did the best I could at that time. Please forgive me, Mom; I don't know what more to say now except that I love you very much. Please forgive me, Mom; I appreciate all you did for me and all the love you gave me. Please forgive me, Mom. Please forgive me, Mom. Please forgive me."

Instructions for seeking forgiveness from others

Step 1. Focus on the person from whom you seek forgiveness, then say or write, "Please forgive me (insert name of that person here), I...." Complete this sentence stating why you are seeking forgiveness. For example: "Please forgive me, Mom; I didn't tell you how much I appreciated you and loved you."

Step 2. Repeat Step 1 again, this time adding another reason why you are seeking forgiveness from that person. For example, "Please forgive me, Mom; I behaved so bratty and spoiled."

Step 3. Repeat this format over and over again, each time completing the sentence by adding a different statement of why you are seeking forgiveness, until you have said all there is to say to that person experientially, and for three consecutive times the words come out simply, "Please forgive me. Please forgive me. Please forgive me." Then experience the release of feeling forgiven and forgiving yourself, even if that person is unable to tell you he or she forgives you.

Couple seeking forgiveness

Whenever possible, seek forgiveness of your partner directly. This can be cleansing and can help bring about renewed intimacy and closeness. Following is an example of what seeking forgiveness can lead to.

I asked Carol and Charles to face each other, establish eye contact, and tell each other what they each wanted to be forgiven for, one at a time. Carol looked at Charles as she began: "I drove you too hard to get ahead. I wanted to prove to my parents that we could make it without their help. I should have gotten a part-time job to help you out. I didn't give you enough affection either. My priorities were all wrong. I love you and I'm sorry. Please forgive me."

Charles' eyes were full of tears as he replied, "I did it. I allowed you to push me. I was feeling very angry, but instead of telling you to lay off, I went out and had an affair. I'm sorry. I know I hurt you. I love you very much. Please forgive me."

After this forgiveness process, I encouraged Carol and Charles to not dig up the past again and to rebuild trust, because trust and love go hand in hand.

Reprogramming yourself through positive affirmations

Many individuals live their entire lives with negative programming: "I'm stupid," "I'm ugly," "I'm unworthy," "I'm no good," "I'm not lovable," "I don't deserve to be happy," "I'll never achieve success." Positive affirmations are nurturing statements that can change the negative messages we send ourselves to positive ones. Because the purpose of positive affirmations is to counteract past negative programming from the past, the messages we give ourselves must speak to our whole being about how we want to be and how we want our lives to be. For example, if in the past we have felt undeserving of happiness, an appropriate affirmation would speak of deserving happiness in words such as, "*I am* the best, and I deserve the best." If we feel incapable of achieving success, our affirmation might be, "*I can* achieve success." If we feel weak or inadequate, our affirmation might be, "*I am* growing stronger each day." If we feel anxious, our affirmation might be, "*I am* feeling more secure and comfortable every day." If we feel overwhelmed, we might affirm, "*I am* feeling capable and in charge of all I have to do." If we feel out of control, we might compose the affirmation, "*I am* in control of my behavior at all times."

Compose your affirmation, in your own words, stating clearly and concisely what you are trying to accomplish. Below are sample affirmations to help guide you in composing your own affirmation:

> ➢ I am relaxing harsh expectations for myself.
> ➢ I am learning to relax and enjoy life.
> ➢ I am healing myself from past pain and grief.
> ➢ I am worthy.
> ➢ I am deserving.
> ➢ I have all I need to attain success.
> ➢ I am continually expanding my personal growth.

- I am successful.
- I am stronger each day.
- I am growing in independence each day.
- I am a feeling and caring person.
- I open myself to love and passion.
- I am open to learning and growing.
- I see myself as a growing person who learns from my experiences.
- I am a good friend to myself.
- I am in control of my actions.
- I am the best I can be.
- I make time for myself and my loved ones.
- I am overcoming my fears.
- I am in the driver's seat of my own life.
- I am a loving parent to myself.
- I am a loving partner.
- I am a loving parent.
- I reach out to others for love and friendship.
- I confront and resolve my problems.
- I share my feelings with my loved ones.
- I give and receive love freely.
- I find love and beauty in the world.
- I am a beautiful person.
- I am more relaxed and comfortable each day.
- I deserve the best that life has to offer, and I will find it.

Empowering affirmations
for men and women

The following affirmations for men and women can be empowering and healing. These affirmations were adapted from Margo Adair's book, *Working Inside Out: Tools for Change.* Fortunately roles for men and women are changing. Women can now demonstrate qualities of personal power, competence, independence, as well as be nurturing to themselves and others. Men need no longer deny the sensitive side of their natures. Men can now be strong, as well as gentle and caring and loving. Neither need be threatened by the other. Now men and women can both be whole and complete as they were meant to be.

Affirmation for women

The emphasis for you now is on reclaiming yourself, on caring for yourself, encouraging yourself, and nourishing yourself. (In the past, the emphasis for women was on doing all this for others.)

Empower yourself and nurture your personal power. Feel yourself as dynamic, capable, and competent, as a creative being, independent, able, strong, and in command. Reclaim your body. Everyone's bodies and everyone's capacities are to be respected.

Affirmation for men

The emphasis for you now is on nourishing yourself, and on healing and relaxing harsh expectations. (In the past, the emphasis for men was on competing and on gaining power over women.)

Heal yourself. Relax your harsh expectations. Encourage the warm, tender, and loving qualities in yourselves. Free yourselves of prior conditioning that told you, "Don't cry, be a man," or "Don't be scared, be a man." Let down your guard. Share and be caring with other men. Create a community of men. Allow competitiveness to ease. There's no need to be the smartest, fastest, biggest, strongest. Free yourself from always being in command, from being the boss, uptight, cold, and lonely. Become more flexible, caring, and compassionate. Express yourself more fully. Create a climate of mutual respect and support.

Kinesthetic tracing of affirmations

An additional learning aid to help you integrate these affirmations is the use of kinesthetic tracing. This method is my adaptation for therapeutic purposes of a special education technique developed by Dr. Grace Fernald and practiced at the Fernald School at UCLA in the 1960s.

Your affirmation should be written on an 8½ x 11 sheet of paper, using the width to allow for large cursive handwriting. Letters should be between 1 to 2 inches high for easy tracing, and written with a black, red, or purple crayon. The touch of the waxy crayon as your index finger slides along the words helps impress your affirmation in your mind.

Trace your affirmation with your index finger six times, while saying it aloud. In this way, you say it, hear it, see it, and actually sense your affirmation kinesthetically. Then close your eyes, visualize your affirmation again, and repeat your affirmation an additional six times to yourself. This process is to be repeated once or twice daily for one week or more until your affirmation becomes part of you.

A note of caution: I introduce the use of affirmations only after clients have worked on underlying problems. The use of affirmations alone, without exploring and resolving problems, is like trying to cover a festering wound with a bandage without first removing the splinter.

Positive affirmations should be used regularly and consistently to bring about desired results. After all, positive reprogramming must counteract years of negative programming, and this takes time.

Creating new beginnings

Over the years, relationships change. Some couples have most of their problems in the beginning of the marriage, others during child-rearing years, and still others after the children are grown. Following are stories of four couples who have all worked diligently on their marriages. Each couple spoke openly and candidly about their problems, how they worked out their difficulties, and what they learned from their experiences. Shuli and Menachem struggled for the first 25 years because of Shuli's intense anger. After she would explode, Menachem would turn inward and sulk, which caused Shuli to feel all the more angry. Finally, in their 25th year, Menachem told her that her severe anger was not acceptable. This caused a major shift in their relationship. Shuli was afraid of losing him and went into therapy. She and Menachem participated in seminars for couples together. At the time I interviewed them, they had been married 36 years, the last 18 of which they agreed were very happy ones. Presently, they are looking forward to celebrating their 50th wedding anniversary next year.

Florence and Mickey's struggles encompassed their first two years together. Florence's immaturity, insecurity, and dependency needs caused Mickey to feel overwhelmed and in need of his own space, which, in turn, caused Florence to feel needy and depressed. Fortunately, I, Florence, was in therapy working on my own issues from childhood and I remained in therapy for 18 months longer after we married. Gradually I worked through my dependency needs and became independent. From then on, Mickey and I have had a magnificent marriage. We recently celebrated our 47th wedding anniversary.

Pete and Connie's struggle encompassed a two-year period. Pete had dreams of becoming an actor but had to face the bitterness, anger, and disappointment when his acting career failed and everything he ever wanted went down the drain. During this period, he had some occasional short-term therapy to help him work through his ambivalence between wanting his bright, talented wife to do well and not wanting to be shown up. With patience and honest communication, they were able to pass through this crisis and set realistic goals for their future together.

Carol and John were separated two years after being married for 20 years. John had struggled with anger and frustration due to unfulfilled expectations, even though Carol catered to all his demands. Finally, John left, but at the time of their interview, they had been reconciled for 12 years. During that time they had both gone for therapy together and individually, John's expectations were more realistic, and their communication skills had improved. John and Carol are very enthusiastic about the future and look forward to spending the rest of their lives together.

All four couples interviewed were committed to their partners and willing to work on their relationships. They were also willing to go for professional help with the goal of growing as individuals and as couples. To couples who are struggling, I want to say: If there is still feeling left for each other, I urge you to work on resolving your problems and consider therapy for yourself and with your partner. If you try and fail to save your relationship, at least you will know you tried. Otherwise, as time goes by, you may deeply regret not even trying. It is my hope that the positive results these couples achieved will inspire you to work on your relationship.

Shuli and Menachem

At the time of this interview, Shuli and Menachem were about ready to celebrate their 36th wedding anniversary. For the first 25 years of their marriage, they struggled with serious problems, which almost caused them to split up. But their commitment to each other and their willingness to work on their relationship enabled them to reach what they now describe as "a marvelous, comfortable, and satisfying stage in our lives." In the interview that follows, Shuli and Menachem explain how they resolved their conflicts together. They have both asked me to use their real names.

Menachem:

"First of all, I think we had a commitment to having a lasting marriage. There was the idea in our minds that we were going to work on it, and that we were committed to being married unless things were totally impossible, which, fortunately, they have never gotten to be. That was one of the things. The other point was that, if we had a very, very severe quarrel, we had the idea that we couldn't go to bed separately."

Shuli:

"We would always go to bed together."

Menachem:

"We'd go to bed together, and sometime during the night, we would try to make up or make love. In other words, not carry it on to the following day. There were certain insights that we gathered through Marriage Encounter. We learned to discuss our feelings with one another and not to disregard each other's feelings. We also both took another group workshop called Lifespring. The ideas I gathered from that were that every person has a diamond inside them, every person has a tremendous amount of worth, and every person sees the world differently. The way other people see the world is of value, and it's not something for you to dismiss.

"There are a lot of things that I admire in Shuli. We view the world differently in certain respects and our personalities are different. Shuli is much more aggressive and more organized than I am. On the other hand, these differences are the cause of my being attracted to her, and sexually we're very compatible. Also, there are certain common interests we share, such as Judaism and prayer, and of course, our children and grandchildren, and friends."

Shuli:

"One of the things I want to say is that we're looking back over 36 years, and what I do now is not what I did 36 years ago. I'm sitting here and thinking: When we were first married, in our very first apartment, our first landlord put a stained glass little thing of two lovebirds into the window because that's how she perceived us. We were very, very deeply in love, and I still am. After 36 years I don't handle problems the way I did then, thank God, because I used to be angry a lot of the time. He was the recipient of a tremendous amount of my anger, and we did quarrel a great deal; but we also had an awful lot of fun together. In fact, in our albums from the early years, we both used to write in 'amidst pain and happiness' because our relationship always had both. Somehow or other, I guess there was more happiness than pain because we always enjoyed each other, always had fun together. Our interests are very similar. Our approach to people and to living is very similar. There's a real commonality of interest shared.

"We had a lot of quarrels. Looking back on it now, I think I had a lot of growing to do. In the early years of our marriage, I used to explode and Menachem would turn inward and sulk; but we never went to bed without making up. I think sex was a very strong bond in the first 25 years. Lifespring, which I went to 20 years ago, was an enormous help for me, in terms of learning more about myself and how I could relate to him. This brought much more satisfaction to both of us. Menachem had reached a point where my behavior was no longer acceptable, my behavior being my severe anger. I'll never forget the day he said that to me. I took him quite seriously and I decided that was it, and I changed.

"There were a lot of things happening at that time: Lifespring, and I had been in therapy, but we always, always talked. There may have been a lot of screaming and shouting but we never let things go. We always discussed what bothered us. That was a very good feeling.

"We haven't had any real fights for so long. It's very different now from how it used to be, a lot calmer. The only thing I miss is that, in the earlier years after we had terrific fights, the making up was wonderful. Now we don't have terrific fights. It's more on an even keel. I'm really glad that we persevered in those early years because I do believe that we are reaping a really wonderful harvest now. We have shared a lot of marvelous, marvelous things together and a lot of pain, but it's been good, really good."

Menachem:

"I think nowadays people see that so many other people are divorced that the possibility of divorce is always there from the very, very beginning; whereas, in my generation, we didn't really see the possibility of divorce. Divorce is now a socially acceptable possibility and people don't stick it out. I remember in our 25th year, we were having a big party to celebrate our 25th wedding anniversary and yet, I remember feeling that we were very, very unhappy. I was wondering whether we would survive through our 26th year. There was so much anger. Obviously, even in that year, there was a commitment to working on our marriage.

"I don't feel people are that way today. Maybe it's good, maybe they don't suffer needlessly all those years. On the other hand, who can tell how it's going to turn out? Like I said, in our 25th year, I had grave doubts, and now I'm tremendously glad that we worked at it because, in the last years, it's been just fabulous.

"What helped our situation turn around was the fact that we gained insight. I attribute a lot of it to Lifespring and to Marriage Encounter and the insight that people are valuable and that the way other people look at the world has validity. Before this, when Shuli, who is very sociable, and I would go to synagogue, afterward she would always want to stay later and talk and talk until she was the last person to leave. I was always railing against her, trying to get her to leave, and finally, I said to myself, you know, this is the way she is and I have to accept the way she is. If I want to leave, then it's up to me to come in a separate car and leave by myself, or else have an agreement beforehand. She's entitled to have her own view of the way the world is constructed. It has validity for her. It doesn't mean that my view is wrong. It's just that she's entitled to do it her way. When you realize this, it's really a great insight. It would be great if someone could teach you all this wisdom beforehand, but it's something that I've gotten through the years."

Shuli:

"Marriage Encounter, which we went to right after our 25th wedding anniversary, has helped us turn around a great number of things. After Marriage Encounter, Menachem changed enormously in terms of being able to express feelings, and so a lot of things that were really not discussed beforehand or were difficult to discuss were much easier. You know, a lot of men won't go, but he took it seriously and he worked at it, and that was enormously to our benefit. I felt the same thing with Lifespring. I got insights from both of those workshops, and other insights in therapy.

"Most of my insights were really understanding myself instead of being unconscious of the way I relate to him. I am much more conscious of who I am. One of the insights that I'm working at much more than Menachem seems to need to work at is to respect his individuality and give him the freedom to be who he really is and to accept him completely. He does treat me that way now. I think that's a wonderful model for me. It's something that I would like to do more. There's also a very fine line between respecting another person's individuality and, let's say, my needs and his needs. It takes a little effort to get a balance between the two, but having a good marriage takes effort. It doesn't just happen.

"Most of my insights have been in terms of how I function and what I really want. I've always wanted this marriage to succeed. So I sometimes say to myself, 'Well what does it need? What will it take?'

"Menachem used to tell me that I was very angry at my father, that all my anger was really directed toward my father and that much of what I said to him was what I really wanted to say to my father. But I would get even angrier when he said that to me because I thought he wasn't taking responsibility for his own behavior. I've turned around 180 degrees on that because he was very right.

"I have changed. I don't feel angry anymore. I have been in therapy with a wonderful woman therapist who has helped me see, to a great extent, that I was very angry at my father and also very angry at my mother. I could never really forgive her for being deaf all of my life and my father for rejecting me. He did reject me.

"I got to the point where I just didn't feel angry anymore, but I also think the impact of Menachem saying, 'This behavior is unacceptable,' shocked me. I will never forget that day. I had broken a stick I was so angry. I whacked the stick on the bed. It was my favorite walking stick. I must have been ready to listen to his words, or else it was the tone of his voice. I remember I went to my therapist and I discussed it with her. I was a little scared after that. I didn't want to lose him.

"Nobody would have known from the outside what was happening, but I knew that he would not take my anger anymore. It meant I really had to learn how to handle it. In a sense, I made a choice. I didn't want to get angry if that meant losing him or losing his love. So I let go of the anger, and that took many years. I also think the birth of our grandson changed me. I just have not been angry."

Menachem:

"What Shuli said is accurate. Her anger is definitely gone. She still gets annoyed and blows up somewhat, but essentially what she said is true. Her raging anger has disappeared. She attributes a lot of it to my saying that her behavior is unacceptable, and I'm sure that's a part of it, but there's more to it than that. I can't help but feel that some sort of insight, some sort of recognition, some sort of being at peace has also taken place.

"It's interesting. I kept a diary at one point on her anger and it decreased from every other day to once every three months, and then it disappeared. I considered her actions and expressions anger if it persisted overnight. Then I would write it down. The most frequent cause of her getting very, very angry was a lack of communication, when I would do something and not communicate it to her in a way that she felt was appropriate. Let's say, for instance, I left the house and went away for half an hour without telling her, or I came home late and didn't call her.

"That is still a difficulty with me. I'm not terribly communicative or talkative. Nonetheless, Shuli has not blown up in the same situations where she used to before. We haven't really had rip-roaring fights in many, many years."

Shuli:

"When Menachem just talked about keeping the diary, that triggered something. I really wasn't aware of how often I got angry. His keeping the diary made me aware of it. I couldn't believe it. I remember saying to myself, 'If I blow up, he's going to write it down, and I don't want him to write it down.' I was very proud of myself when he didn't write it down for a whole week or a whole month. We did analyze it. It was very interesting. Every time I got angry, it was because of what he would call 'noncommunication.' It was when he would withdraw into himself and I couldn't reach him. My continual expression was 'I'm talking to a wall,' or 'I'm talking to a statue and you're not really here.' That always triggered enormous, enormous frustration and anger in me. Now he does that much, much less. I've learned that, when he does it, I say, 'Please, I need you to be here.' In other words, rather than screaming and yelling, 'Why aren't you here?' I'd make him aware of the fact. That was always the reason for my blowup. It was because I felt unlistened to. My mother was deaf; the whole connection is very close there."

"And my father wasn't there either. I'm talking to him and he's totally not there, totally absorbed in whatever problem it was and not sharing it with me. You know, I felt so left out. The other expression I always used to say to Menachem was, 'I feel lonely.' I haven't said that in a long time. I also used to say, 'It's impossible to think that I'm living with somebody and sleeping with somebody and feeling lonely.' But we've worked on that and I have found a way to reach him without screaming and yelling."

As this interview came to a close, I congratulated Shuli and Menachem for their growth and courage and told them that they are an inspiration.

In the year 2000, Shuli and Menachem look forward with great joy to celebrating their 50th wedding anniversary. The latest update I received from them, just after their 49th anniversary, was: "It keeps getting better and better."

Florence and Mickey

Most of the problems my husband, Mickey, and I had occurred during the first two years of our marriage. At 22, I seemed very grown up and independent, but inside, I was still insecure and needy. Fortunately, I had already been in therapy for two years when I met Mickey and I continued therapy for two additional years after we were married. I was working through painful old feelings from my childhood and this took me a long time. I would get moody, depressed, and overly sensitive sometimes, and Mickey reacted by distancing himself from me. He was manifesting his own feelings of disappointment. I was suddenly not the smiling, independent woman he thought he was marrying. Instead, I was behaving like an insecure child.

We were very fortunate to have survived those early years and remain together. I was so immature in certain respects, as was he. I am very grateful to him for sticking by me while I grew up. Since that time, our relationship has grown increasingly magnificent through the years. We recently celebrated our 47th wedding anniversary and look forward to our 50th.

Following is a transcript of an interview I taped 13 years ago in which we reflected on our thoughts during our difficult years and talked about our present lives together.

Florence:

"Well, my love, here we are sitting across from each other, married almost 34 years. We've been through a lot together, and even though the first couple of years were very difficult, we managed to work through them and stay together. Now, even after all these years, when I look at you, I feel a wonderful, warm glow of love. You are still my sweetheart."

Mickey:

"And you are mine."

Florence:

"I want to ask you, though, how did you really stick out those couple of difficult years? I mean, I must have been a tremendous disappointment for you. I was very emotional and still needed therapy very badly. Some husbands might have just walked away or bailed out. What was going on in your mind and in your feelings that allowed you to stick it out?"

Mickey:

"I think once a husband and wife have made a commitment, it's a commitment for life. When you stop to think, 'Who does one really have?' You realize we have all sorts of relatives, but they are involved with their own family problems. We have friends and acquaintances, but they are all involved with their families. We have children, but eventually they go off on their own and have their own lives. So, in effect, we only really have each other. The bottom line is: It's only us and we've given a commitment. We have to make whatever effort we can to help each other to improve our relationship, grow together, and do whatever we can to make it work."

Florence:

"So, it was your commitment? You must have also had some faith that things were going to improve, otherwise it would have been very, very discouraging."

Mickey:

"Well, loving someone, you can't explain why, it's just there. When it comes to our relationship, there were certain traits you had that I admired and respected and loved. If there were also a few areas that were not working, then that was no reason for breaking up a marriage, because of a few dark spots. So we tried to work on those areas and do whatever we could to grow in those areas."

Florence:

"You knew that I was in therapy when we met and that I was working on my problems. But if I hadn't been in therapy, would you perhaps have had more doubts about the future?"

Mickey:

"I think, in those days, I wasn't too oriented toward psychologists or psychiatry or therapy of any type. It was not within the realm of my understanding or experience. So I didn't have feelings, one way or the other. All I knew was that, if there was a problem, we had to work it out by whatever means there were. I, of course, had my own sets of problems, so I wasn't an expert on how to resolve your problems. I had my own to work out, too."

Florence:

"Just this afternoon, as a matter of fact, we saw a movie called *Always*. It was about a couple who were divorced and they were going to be signing their final papers, but ended up spending the weekend together. The reason she had left her husband was because she didn't feel happy all the time when she was married to him. Yet, when she was separated those two years, she wasn't feeling happy all the time either.

"I think some people have the notion that they want to find someone who's going to make them happy all the time. That's not something that someone else can do for you. Do you agree with that?"

Mickey:

"Yes, sometimes you can't appreciate happiness unless you've experienced unhappiness. There are going to be ups and downs in any relationship, even by oneself, or with a mate, a family, even with other nations of the world. Things happen that are not acceptable for whatever reason and you just have to work those problems out in the best interests of everyone."

Florence:

"You aren't really a critical person, but I remember how very hurt and sensitive I used to be when I used to think you were angry with me about something. At such times, I used to feel rejected and get depressed over it. For the first couple of years, I remember there were some pretty bleak weekends. Do you remember that?"

Mickey:

"No, I don't remember that. Not so many years later."

Florence:

"I'm so happy that you were willing to stick it out and that you had the patience to wait through those difficult years. It would have been just terrible if we had split up, lost each other, and missed the chance to enjoy each other all these years. I think that our marriage has turned out to be beautiful."

Mickey:

"Well, you may have felt more negative and insecure about the situation than I did. You might have felt very insecure, right? You were probably more inclined to exaggerate how you thought I would feel, when I really didn't feel that bad about it. And you were feeling so negative about yourself that you exaggerated many situations."

Florence:

"Now that so many years have passed, and we've raised three wonderful children, and we have gorgeous grandchildren, what hints do you have for couples who are having problems?"

Mickey:

"I think, aside from loving each other, partners really have to like each other. Sometimes you can't help loving a person, but that person might be terrible for you. It's nice when you can really like and admire the one you love and feel at ease and comfortable. Communication is very important. If one says something or does something that disturbs the other, it has to be brought to that person's attention, letting him or her know it hurt your feelings, instead of hiding your anger, because otherwise it just piles up until the big explosion. Get it out there as soon as possible! Then it only hurts for a few seconds or hours, and then it's over with. Communicate anything that is bothering you.

"I think if one person is very sensitive, the other should respect that sensitivity and ask when these things can be discussed and talked over."

Florence:

"You know, I've really learned so much from you. One very important thing I learned was to become independent and develop my own interests. You have always encouraged me to do that. I think that otherwise I would have been hanging onto you. At first, I took it as a sign of rejection when you wanted to go off sailing on your own, and I couldn't go because I get seasick, or you went off working on an archeological excavation, and I didn't want to do that. Instead, you encouraged me to do some things on my own, and it's been wonderful. We're together a lot and we each have interests of our own. It means we can both enjoy our lives to the fullest. Just because one partner doesn't like to do something, doesn't mean that the other should give up doing that. So I really want to thank you for that."

Mickey:

"I didn't want to drag you by the hand through life. I wanted us to walk hand in hand through the meadows, each feeling good about ourselves and good about each other."

Florence:

"Do you know how many men want to keep their wives barefoot and pregnant, so to speak? That's another thing I so admire about you. You have never been possessive of me. You've always trusted me. I talk to some women clients who tell me that every time they go to the market, their husband makes a remark, 'Who did you talk to?' 'Why were you there so long?' or 'Who did you meet?' I just couldn't live that way. I think I have been a little possessive of you, although I hope not that stifling or restricting. I think I've improved on that."

Mickey:

"I'm very thankful to you for being so supportive of me developing myself. It's very important that a couple help each other to grow and achieve maturity. That way, they can grow together and enjoy each other even more."

Florence:

"I'm very glad we're both taking care of our health, eating healthy, and exercising, so we can look forward to a long, healthy life together. I'm especially pleased that you take care of yourself, because so many men just don't watch themselves at all. You keep your weight down and you eat right and you exercise. I don't want to be a widow."

Mickey:

"Well, I wouldn't want you turning me in for a later model."

Florence:

"I'll never turn you in. You're the model I want forever."

Connie and Pete

Connie and Pete were married six and a half years at the time of this interview. Together, they developed an effective way of relating and communicating with one another. In the transcribed interview that follows, they tell how they dealt with a major crisis, relying on their strong faith in God, on trust in one another, and on open and honest communication.

Pete:

"I'll start with some basic rules that we developed. One is that, if we are arguing, we will not leave the room without completing the discussion. We won't turn our back on the other person and just leave the room. And that's very, very hard. Because there are times you just want to throw up your hands and say, 'You're hopeless. I'm leaving. I'm going to go take a walk and cool off.' We find that we end up hurting the other and don't really resolve things when we come back. So we've made that rule. We also try to speak in 'I feel' statements. For instance, 'When you did this, I felt...,' rather than saying 'You're doing this to me.' We believe that we would never do anything to consciously hurt each other. That's one we have to work on, because we're all human, you know, and we want revenge."

Connie:

"That's our basic assumption that we try to live by."

Pete:

"It makes the conflict a little easier to bear and a little easier to resolve coming from that basis: 'This person doesn't want to hurt me. This person wants my best and has by best interests at heart.'"

Connie:

"Some people are just good communicators and it would be easier for them to have a good marriage, because communication is so important. But we came from a place where both of our backgrounds were so totally different. I came from a family where we got our feelings out. Everybody screamed and yelled, but we weren't careful about whether we hurt someone or not. We just expressed it and that was the way I functioned. When I first met Pete, I saw him perform on stage. I saw him sing and I was very impressed, but on one-on-one communication, he literally couldn't carry on a conversation. It was like pulling teeth to get him to express feelings. I jokingly told him that, to other people, he might look like an oyster; but I knew there was a pearl inside. I kept trying to get him to express himself.

"We started out as friends before we started courting one another. During our friendship stage, we had to really practice talking to each other. I'm the one who will force the issue. If I need to know what he's feeling or why he's acting in such a way, I will just pursue it. I will not stop until I know and sometimes he can't handle that. In our relationship, we started with Pete coming from a very noncommunicative or nonverbal, repressive home situation. This has caused problems between my in-laws and me. If they don't like something, they don't talk to you. They ignore you and they just silently punish you and assume that you're going to figure out what you did wrong."

Pete:

"There was a lot of nonverbal communication, but I knew exactly what was being said."

Connie:

"I'm the one who will just go up and say, 'What did I do? Why do I deserve this kind of treatment?' At one point, during our courtship, we were having real problems. We were trying to decide whether we should break up or commit more to the relationship, and at that point, we had a discussion. I remember, we were sitting in the car and I was crying so hard the car was shaking. The discussion basically was, 'Is it worth expressing your feelings even if the other person gets hurt?' Pete's feeling was, 'I don't want to say things because they might hurt you.' And my feeling was, 'Instead of wondering if the other person's mad at you or wondering if you've done something to offend him, it is worth sharing honest feelings and working through the hurt.' And I can be persuasive."

Pete:

"I think, in sharing honest feelings, there has to be a balance. You can fall into the trap of sharing honest feelings, just saying what's on your mind, but what happens is that you have no consideration for the other person if you're not kind. If you can remember to be kind and say things in a way that is going to help them receive it, then I think you'll be more effective."

Connie:

"That's one of the things I learned from Pete, because my family members were not polite to each other, even though we were expressive. So, to give his parents some credit, they did teach him to be very respectful and courteous. That is something he has brought to our communication process that has really helped. We will think things through and say, 'Wait a minute, I'm feeling something. Let me think of how to say it in an appropriate way that won't push buttons and stop the communication.'"

Pete:

"A little diplomacy."

Connie:

"We met in my freshman year of college. We got married in our junior year, and we graduated together a year later. I would say that, probably the thing that most influenced our relationship and made our relationship possible is our commitment to Jesus Christ."

Pete:

"And it's what keeps us together."

Connie:

"Yeah. Because otherwise I don't think we ever would have survived."

Pete:

"I believe that opposites attract, but let's be realistic. We were so different. I didn't even like her for two whole years."

Connie:

"You liked me."

Pete:

"I mean I didn't like you, boyfriend-girlfriend. I liked you, you know, as a friend."

Connie:

"Of course, I weighed 40 pounds more than you do now."

Pete:

"That's true. We felt God's hand in our relationship, putting us together and helping us grow together and even getting us to the point of marriage. From then on that has really kept us together. Now, you know, we're considering working in the ministry together. It's so exciting. We really like being together. I don't like being apart from her. And we work best, I think, and are most productive when we're together. I don't know if every couple could say that, but it's true for us."

Connie:

"I was just going to say that the changes that have taken place in us from the day we met are so incredible in every way. We went to our college reunion, and one guy came up to Pete and Pete said, 'Oh, you remember Connie?' And the guy said, 'Well, what happened to the other Connie you were dating?' That guy didn't even realize that I was the same person. My appearance had changed so much, and my demeanor, everything."

Pete:

"Connie was really brassy back then, a very forceful personality."

Connie:

"Unpolished brass."

Pete:

"Yeah, Yeah. Diamond in the rough."

Connie:

"There's a scripture that says, 'Work out your own salvation with fear and trembling, for it is the Lord who is at work within you.' It's God working in us to accomplish His will. One scripture that we go by is, 'Don't let the sun go down on your anger.' Another is, 'Be angry, but do not sin.' So we don't. If we're having a fight, we deal with it. We don't go to bed angry. It's the balance of God and ourselves. We know we have our part. If we don't obey and do our part, God's not going to magically give us a wonderful marriage."

Pete:

"There's something I want to bring up that's very important, especially in our culture that places so much emphasis on success: It's going for your dream. For men in pursuit of their careers, it's so easy to lose sight of what's important. What was important on our wedding day is still important, and that is togetherness. I think it's the man's place to say: 'I want to have time with you. And I'm going to arrange my life so that you are a priority. Your needs come first.' You've got to lay down your life and make the sacrifices to make sure that she is fulfilled in every possible way. For a lot of men, that stops at being a provider. I think it goes on to being a companion, being a friend, being interested in her interests, holding her up, and helping her to be the best she can be.

"We're excited for each other's personal growth. Like I mentioned before, I like being around Connie. I think it's important that you never fall out of love with someone, but also that you don't fall out of liking them. I like being around her and I like being interested in what she's interested in."

Connie:

"I like hearing this."

Pete:

"In relation to her personal growth issue: I like to see her grow and see her develop, when she has an idea, to see it grow and develop and blossom and, if I can help, that's great. I think many men feel threatened if they are not personally growing or not succeeding. I had to go through this when my career was going nowhere and she was working on a book. She was succeeding. I had to deal with that. We communicated. I was honest with her. I was in tears and said, 'Look, I am so afraid that I'm going to wake up some day and you're going to make it and I'm not going to.' It's just terribly frightening for me. Maybe it's the male psyche, maybe it's just inbred. I don't know. We're people who do not hesitate to go to counselors when we need counsel and I think that's really important. Whenever we have a problem that's too big for us to solve, we find someone we can counsel with. We've found a lot of people along the way, and in one instance, I found some good counseling that helped me. I've felt threatened on and off, and each time I've dealt with it when it comes up."

Connie:

"That's one of the tensions in our marriage. I don't know how to put this delicately. When I was in school, I was labeled as mentally gifted. There were special programs for mentally gifted. When you're singled out as being bright, the kids tend to look at you, and I did not want to be looked at like a bookworm. So I rebelled. I worked so hard to get Cs instead of As. It was a theme throughout my life, where teachers would get so angry with me and say, 'You could do so much.' After I became a Christian, I felt a real obligation to use what God had given me. I figured He'd given it to me for a reason. I'm still very tempted to be mediocre in order to be liked. There's nothing in the world that hurts me more than to think somehow I would make Pete feel inadequate. Actually, the idea is not to compare ourselves to each other, but that's not realistic. The guy I was in a relationship with before I met Pete was threatened and he would just tear me down and ridicule anything I attempted. It worked. I stopped all my pursuits. I really respect Pete's courage in saying he feels these feelings, but in no way does he want me to stop pursuing to my best."

Pete:

"There's the paradox of wanting the best for her and being so excited about what she can do. It's just like playing Pygmalion and then not wanting to be shown up. I want some measure of success also. Men place all their self-image in their jobs, whereas women do not. What's helped me, I think, was just growing up, maturing, and coming to realize who I am, and saying to myself, 'That's okay. She's someone different and that's okay too.' It's a struggle that I deal with from time to time, but it's become less apparent."

Connie:

"As you've become more confident, it's less of a threat."

Pete:

"My earliest memories were of watching old MGM musicals and just dreaming of growing up and being on stage. From earliest childhood, all I wanted to do was perform."

Connie:

"And you were very talented!"

Pete:

"I was good. I was really good."

Connie:

"Excellent."

Pete:

"I went to so many auditions and took so many classes. I gave it a try and it just wasn't coming. Also, I began to realize that there wasn't a living to be made. When the baby came, I realized I did have to take a full-time job, and I went through a real crisis. I went through a period of mourning, because I had lost my identity. I didn't know who I was. Everything I'd ever wanted just went down the drain. I think Connie's love for me and my faith in God got me through. I really do. It was a very, very difficult time for almost two years. I didn't want to watch television or go to a movie because it would remind me of that kind of feeling. I just had to face the bitterness and the anger and the disappointment and say, 'God, I don't know why You did this, why You allowed it to happen. But you're God. That's why you do these things. You're in control.' I just wanted to be happy again."

Connie:

"There was that tension of you looking for people to blame. It would be very easy to blame the baby for this loss. What we settled on helped us. We just came to a point of saying, 'God is not going to waste these talents,' because I look at Pete and his musical ability and his performing ability and it is obviously a talent, it's a gift.

We don't know when or where those gifts are going to be used. We're just going to put that back in God's hands and go on with our lives."

Pete:

"I think what helped me through that time was Connie's support. She anguished with me, she mourned with me, and she would just say, 'Look, if there was any way, I'd do it. I would do anything it would take.' She would encourage me by saying, 'Look, I don't think your talent is going to be wasted. I think, someday you'll be doing something.' I don't hurt anymore, which is a miracle. I'm so thankful that life goes on. I've discovered a whole world of talents and abilities that I never would have known. Being the manager that I am and having the job that I have and then going on into this new thing that we're planning, the ministry, I never would have developed those. We plan to go into ministry together and work with youth. In a nutshell, we would like to be a consulting team to youth groups that are striving to develop."

Connie:

"I feel like we've been asked to give up the very things we've desired, only to find that God gave them back to us in ways we never imagined. I mean, this is like everything we've wanted."

John and Carol

After 20 years of marriage, Carol and John were separated for two years and were planning to divorce. The following interview reveals what led up to their separation and subsequent reconciliation and how they have been working on their marriage together since their reconciliation. Although they almost lost each other, at the time of this interview, 12 years after they got back together, they were looking forward to achieving the most intimate relationship humanly possible.

Carol:

"I remember the incident. We were coming home from somewhere, we were discussing something, and John got very angry about what I said. He left that night. It was a matter of poor communication at the time, maybe not sharing everything and not sharing what we were feeling. Before that, I didn't recognize the problems that we were having. As a result of the separation, we both had counseling and were both in group therapy. It took us a long time to work out many of our problems, which we obviously have done."

John:

"I think our problems went back to almost the inception of our relationship when we met each other. We were not communicating and we were assuming a lot about each other. I had a lot of expectations about our relationship. I took a lot for granted, of what a relationship should be, and I made demands on Carol without regard for her. I didn't question or find out whether she was aware of what my feelings meant to me. When my expectations weren't met, I demanded that they be met, not verbally or physically, but just in our relationship. Carol tried to satisfy what I demanded, whether she agreed or disagreed. I think, in the long run, my demands and her wanting to comply with my demands caused a failure in our relationship.

"I think there was a lot of frustration involved and most of it had to do with a lack of communication. So when we did part, it was with a lot of anger and a lot of vindictiveness on my part. I felt that I had been wronged and exploited. That anger continued for many, many months. When we did get back together again, it took a lot of hard work. As Carol mentioned, we went to counseling, together and individually, and we are still working very hard.

"I would like to say that it wasn't always downhill from the time we met. There was a time in our early married life that we used to try to communicate to a very high degree. We decided together that we would discuss every day the events of that day, thinking that it would help us communicate, not so much because of what took place that day, but basically to create a certain intimacy that we were hoping for. Apparently it wasn't too effective at that time, because about 20 years later we separated."

Carol:

"During our separation we did see each other. We had to see each other because we had three children. There had to be communication with the kids, and eventually, we were either going to group therapy or seeing a counselor together during that time. When we saw each other it wasn't always agreeable or compatible. We both had a lot of anger. I had hopes of getting back together, but eventually recognized that it would most likely end in divorce. That's the way I began to think, near the end. I couldn't allow myself to be hurt either way."

John:

"I was convinced we would not get back together. I was full of anger and animosity. I felt that I had wasted my life in terms of our relationship. It wasn't until we were in counseling that I realized that a good deal of the anger I had toward Carol was misdirected and that some of that anger had to do with the demands that I had made. Her compliance also caused me to be angry and caused her to be angry. Some of that anger was directed at me in an unconscious way, but I didn't realize it at the time.

"I didn't want to get back together. I felt happy and very productive about that time. I always respected Carol, even through my anger. I felt I would never meet another woman with the qualities that I admired so much about Carol. However, emotionally, I couldn't deal with sharing my feelings with her or having her share her feelings with me. I felt that although Carol had a lot of qualities that I respected and admired, we were incompatible on an aesthetic level.

"When I met Carol, she had lost her mother and father, and she was independent. I liked that in Carol, but even though she worked and was a good student and was independent, I had this paternal feeling toward her like she couldn't get along without me. I guess that is my little machismo from my generation, or maybe just the way I am. When we separated, it was important to me that we communicate in terms of our children. I wanted to do the best I could for my children. I also wanted to do the best I could for Carol, because I had this feeling that she needed me, even though I wasn't there. So I used to see Carol. Once in a while, we would meet and have a bite to eat together or I'd come over to visit the children and we'd say a few words. It was a little strained. One night in particular, we were having dinner in a local place, just she and I, and I remember crying because I was happy and sad at the same time. As I mentioned, I was happy about the separation, but I realized that I had a great deal of love for Carol and my feelings, at that moment, were very ambivalent. I felt very frightened by those feelings. When legal things occurred, it was a little more difficult to communicate with Carol, and sometimes when we didn't agree on the children; we had a lot of difficulty because neither one of us would compromise.

"When we were going for counseling, Carol was serious about getting back together. I just wanted to find out what it was all about. I was going to vent without any obligations to return. And you know, by going to counseling, I found out a lot about myself and a lot about Carol. Some of it was scary as I realized that I was a lot less than perfect and that I couldn't make the kinds of demands on Carol that I had been making."

Carol:

"I think he was jealous. He knew I was going out. We spent some time together and talked about it. He moved back home, and afterward he really wasn't sure he wanted to be there. He didn't feel right about it and he moved out again for a week or 10 days. Then he came home and he's been home ever since. After he came home we continued in counseling and therapy for a few years."

John:

"I had come to pick up our children one day. We had made some arrangements of when I'd see the children. I could come at those times and not exploit Carol by coming anytime I wanted to. After all, she had her life. This one day I'd come to pick up the children, and Carol seemed quite upset.

"Carol told me she'd met a man who, it turned out, was married, and he did not tell her. Carol was very sad about it, because apparently she liked this person. I became so incensed with the immorality of what this man had done. When we were separated and I dated, I would let everybody know immediately that I was not divorced, not a single man. I felt Carol had been exploited by this man and I was very angered by it. I said immediately to Carol, 'Don't worry. I'll take care of it,' still going back to that need I had to be very paternal and very protective of Carol. Carol said, 'No, don't.' But I did anyway.

"To this day, I felt that she wanted me to take care of it, or she wouldn't have told me the story. But, anyway, I made this man squirm and I was very happy about that. I was upset at what had happened to Carol and I said to myself, 'If I'm not around, who knows what's going to happen?' That's what I told myself. What I really felt for Carol was a great deal of love, and I missed her a lot.

"So I came to Carol and I asked her if she would take me back. She said she would think about it. When she said that to me, I panicked. I literally panicked. I begged her to take me back. I said, 'You know, I can't live like this.' So she took me back, and as soon as I got back, I went into a depression. I asked myself, 'Did I overreact? Did I make a bad decision? Why am I here?' I put all this energy into this separation, and suddenly, I went into a depression. I just used to walk around in a daze all of the time.

"Finally, after a few months of that, I came to Carol one day and I said, 'I can't stay here any longer, I have to leave.' But I found out it was something I had created myself. I created that whole scenario. I didn't want to be here. I wasn't ready to come home, whatever that means now. So I told her, I was leaving and she said to me, 'If you leave, you will not come back.' And I left anyway."

Carol:

"And he came back."

John:

"I was gone for about a week or two and had an apartment and I just realized that that wasn't it. Where I wanted to be was with Carol. That's where I felt calm. That's where I felt safe. That was the person with whom I wanted to be. I loved Carol. Even in my depression, she was able to appease me and calm me and she was the most giving human being I'd ever met. If she could have put up with me over that period of time under those circumstances, I realized that rejecting her and rejecting our relationship at that time would have been the greatest mistake I'd ever made. So I came to Carol again and she said, 'I'll think about it.' This time she let me wait for a few days."

Carol:

"A few hours. I don't remember."

John:

"So that was how we got back together. Then, from that time on, both of us truly gave counseling more than lip service. We really did it together. We tried to fulfill all the things that we wanted for ourselves and for each other and tried to eliminate all these destructive behavior characteristics that caused our relationship's demise. The result is that now I've been working on it pretty hard. Things are not easy all the time. There are times when we really have some serious differences of opinion and times when our feelings just aren't together; and even though we still have that, we have had a more fulfilling relationship during the last 10 years than we had in the first 20. We share a lot more, we have a lot more honesty.

"I'd like to point out something that's apparent to all of us, but we don't always respond to it: Life is not a utopian experience. If we try to attain perfection we will be in for disappointment. We should try to search for realistic values and goals in our life and in our relationships. We have to realize that all of us have different perceptions, and our partner sees things differently and has a different perspective than we do. To one, a beautiful sunset might mean just the colors; to the other, a beautiful sunset might mean the shape of the clouds. They're both beautiful and they both have to be appreciated by each other. It's the same for a relationship. We can both see beautiful things, and yet, not see the same thing at all. Sharing helps create a closer, more understanding, more tolerant relationship."

Healing troubled relationships often requires healing ourselves. When we feel good about ourselves, we make better partners. The goal of the three forgiveness processes is to release pain and torment from the past and allow forgiveness and peace to enter. The purpose of this section on reprogramming through positive affirmations is to counteract years of negative programming and enhance our self-image and self-esteem. The section on creating new beginnings contains interviews with couples whose devotion and perseverance serves to inspire struggling couples to work on their relationships and seek professional help when they need to. The next chapter will discuss how therapy can help and where help can be found.

CHAPTER 8

When You Can't Do It Yourself

Not all relationships can be saved, but there are many that can be if couples go for help in time. Couples with serious problems often feel a sense of helplessness and hopelessness and give up. They believe that if they can't work it out themselves, no one else can do it for them. They're right—no one can do it *for* them. But a good marriage counselor or therapist can *help them* do it themselves.

Sometimes it takes a serious crisis for partners to be willing to take a good look at themselves and at their relationship. A time of crisis is an excellent time for growing. Marriage counselors and therapists do much more than rescue marriages. They encourage both partners to grow as individuals, whether or not they choose to stay together.

How counseling can help

The three true anecdotes that follow demonstrate how powerful counseling or therapy can be in helping tear barriers down. Three couples came to me for short-term marriage counseling. In each case, a divorce seemed inevitable.

One task in therapy is to explore roots of feelings and problems. In the case of Greg and Julie, Greg's inability to love deeply stemmed from the death of his little sister and his breaking up with the girl he loved in college. He had unconsciously resolved never to love again because the loss of a loved one was too painful. In John and Lindy's case, John's short temper, which was destroying their marriage, stemmed from his feelings of helplessness and powerlessness as a teenager in the courtroom when his father was on trial. In the case of Cathy and Ted, Cathy's trapped feelings stemmed from her seeing her mother's terrible life being married to Cathy's alcoholic father.

These discoveries were only first steps for Greg, John, and Cathy in working through old feelings that were interfering with their present relationships. Therapy is a fantastic process that can transform lives. I know, because therapy transformed mine from night into day. Without it, I probably would not have married and I certainly would not have become a therapist or written this book.

Greg and Julie

Greg spoke first. "I want this divorce. I'm not happy being married." He explained how trapped he felt getting married in the first place. He had never gotten over it.

"He just doesn't want to be married," Julie responded. "He might just as well go on ahead and get the divorce."

Greg was still torn. He cited so many reasons why he should want to stay married. His wife was lovely and loving. He had beautiful children and a comfortable home, but he just wasn't happy. They had both suffered a lot as a result. The divorce loomed heavily over their heads. Two more months and it would be final. What was there to do? Greg wasn't happy and he couldn't help how he felt. As a marriage counselor, I began to think about this situation. Many questions came to mind: What was the real problem? What was the important ingredient missing for Greg? Why all this ambivalence? He had chased her and begged her to marry him, yet as the wedding approached, he wanted out. Why was he holding back then? Why was he still holding back? Why hadn't he been able to give Julie a full commitment? Why couldn't he love Julie deeply?

I began sharing some of these thoughts with this couple. I told them there appeared to be something important missing for Greg, that one most-important ingredient that makes all the difference in a relationship. He appeared to have everything else: a successful career, a beautiful family, health, all the good things, except the ability to love deeply, and to be deeply, emotionally involved with Julie. I explained why some people hold back. It may seem too risky. It involves being vulnerable and the possibility of getting hurt. Unfortunately this kind of defensiveness condemns a person to being alone.

I asked Greg if he was willing to explore why he might be resisting loving Julie deeply. He was willing to try, so I encouraged him to allow the thoughts to come, not to hold back or censure them, even if they seemed silly or irrelevant. At first he said he couldn't think of any reason. I encouraged him to take more time to see what thoughts might come to his mind. He began thinking about losing his little sister when he was a child. He remembered crying for weeks after her death. He began crying now, just thinking about it, and he wiped back his tears. Next he thought about the girl he had loved in college. When they split up, it took him months to get over it.

Greg asked me, "Why is it important to love someone deeply? Isn't that for childish, insecure people who have to hang onto somebody?"

My reply was, "No. I believe it is for people who are secure enough to risk being vulnerable."

Greg said that he has always felt something really important was missing in his life, but he never knew what it was. Maybe this was it. I reemphasized that deep love and closeness with another person involves reaching out, not holding back. It means taking a risk by allowing oneself to be vulnerable. Making a total commitment to another person takes real courage.

Greg said he had a lot of thinking to do about all of this. He was able to see the relationship between the pain of losing his sister and his first love and his reluctance to allow himself to love Julie.

He said, "I hope this wall I built up will melt away. I know I have a wonderful wife. I have a lot of thinking to do."

This couple came back the following week. Greg said he had decided to drop the divorce. He said he was feeling much more positive about Julie. Now they were ready to work on their relationship. This couple probably would have split up and Greg would have taken his problem along with him into other relationships. Instead, they both looked forward to reconciling.

John and Lindy

The second couple presented a different challenge. A barrier to closeness had to be confronted. John came in alone the first time.

"We love each other, but we just can't get along. My wife is divorcing me. Lindy's tired of my short fuse." John explained that he has a terrible temper, so many things make him angry. He wished he wouldn't be like that, but that was the way he reacted and the way he was.

What could be done? This was John's third marriage. He loved Lindy but his anger was ruining their marriage. As a marriage counselor, I asked myself, "Why was he so angry?" That appeared to be the key question.

"Why are you so angry?" I asked him.

"I don't know why. I always react that way."

"Would you be willing to find out why?"

John was willing, so I asked him to relax, even close his eyes for a moment, and see what thoughts would come when I asked him, "Why are you so angry?"

No thoughts were coming. Then he started thinking about that day in the courtroom when his father was on trial. He felt so helpless and powerless to defend his father. He remembered running out of the courtroom. He thought about all the fights he got into at school afterward trying to defend his father and about all the kids he hit in the face. He started to cry, actually reliving the tragic experience.

His wife, Lindy, accompanied him to the next conference. Things seemed to be improving, they reported. There were many problems to work on and they were ready and willing to do so. Now this couple could work toward creating a new marriage together.

Cathy and Ted

The third couple presented yet another challenge. Cathy wanted the divorce. She described feeling trapped in an unhappy marriage, like being caught in a big web. She explained that she wasn't just divorcing Ted, but also Ted's parents who were very controlling. Cathy described Ted as a quiet, rather mild man. She had the feeling that she was doing things to please everyone but herself. She felt guilty about hurting Ted but she had decided to get out of this marriage.

I asked myself why Cathy felt so trapped. Ted was willing to work on their problems. He assured her he would see to it that his parents were less meddling and controlling, now that he knew how upsetting it was for her. He was also willing to go for help for their sexual problem.

Cathy shook her head. "No, nothing would help now." She just wanted the divorce.

"Why do you feel so trapped?" I asked her. "You mentioned it was like being caught in a big web. Would you be willing to examine those feelings?"

Cathy reluctantly said she'd try. I asked her to relax and see what thoughts came to her mind when she thought of feeling trapped or being caught in a web. Cathy began to think about her mother and the terrible kind of life she and her mother had with her alcoholic father. "And my mother stayed and didn't leave him." For Cathy, marriage meant being stuck in a miserable. situation or being trapped. As a child, she had resolved that she wouldn't be like her mother and stay in a bad marriage. She began to see the relationship then and now.

The session was coming to an end. I asked her what she wanted to see happen this week in terms of her husband and herself. She said that Ted had been pressuring her to reconcile. This made her feel very guilty, especially when he sent flowers or letters and when he called her or came over. She asked him not contact her this week at all. If she wanted to, she would call him. Ted agreed to abide by her wishes as the session ended.

This couple returned the following week. They reported that they had seen each other for dinner once and that Cathy had called him a few times during the week just to talk to him. Cathy said she wasn't sure what she wanted to do. The couple explored the possibility of working out a reconciliation. Cathy said she would like to think about this and return the next week. By the following week the couple had reconciled.

Finding help

Licensed mental health professionals are available in most areas of the United States. I suggest couples look for licensed professionals who specialize in working with couples, rather than solely with individuals. Being seen together can give couples the advantage of being able to expand communication between partners. Each partner can also be seen separately at times at the discretion of the therapist.

Even when therapy does not lead to reconciliation, it can help couples separate more smoothly. One important advantage of therapy is that, even when a couple decides to separate, each partner has the chance to examine his or her own part in making the relationship what it was. This will help each partner to grow and learn from his or her own mistakes and experiences and help them avoid falling into similar patterns later on. For this alone, counseling or therapy is well worthwhile.

Professional associations

The following professional associations can provide information regarding licensed mental health professionals in your area:

American Association of Marriage and Family Therapy
1133 15th St., NW
Ste. 300
Washington, DC 20005
(202) 452-0109

American Psychiatric Association
1400 K St., NW
Washington, DC 20005
(202) 682-6000

American Psychological Association
750 First St., NE
Washington, DC 20002
(202) 336-5500

Association of Family and Conciliation Courts
329 W. Wilson
Madison, WI 53703
(608) 251-4001

Alliance for Children and Families
11700 West Lake Park Dr.
Milwaukee, WI 53224
(800) 221-2681

National Association of Social Workers, Inc.
50 Broadway
10th Floor
New York, NY 10004
(212) 668-0050

Community resources

Emergency help and support for serious emotional or mental problems can be found through your county's mental health department. Shelters for battered partners are available in many communities, and local police departments also give assistance in situations involving domestic violence. Self-help support groups such as Alcoholics Anonymous, Over-Eaters Anonymous, Batters Anonymous, Weight Watchers, and Gamblers Anonymous are available in many communities for specific problem areas. In addition to the above-mentioned resources, many clergy are trained in pastoral counseling and can be of assistance in either providing counseling themselves or in making referrals for help in the community.

CHAPTER 9

Putting It
All Into
Perspective

Do-It-Yourself Conflict Resolution for Couples contains a full spectrum of options for reducing conflict in relationships. I have done my part; the rest is in your hands. A loving, lasting relationship is priceless, well worth whatever efforts are necessary. Putting it all into perspective, I would say that conflict resolution is most possible under the following conditions:

➢ When we can tolerate imperfections in our partner and ourselves.

➢ When we can respect differences of feeling and opinion in our partner.

➢ When we can tolerate some difficult times without giving up.

➢ When we can apologize if we make mistakes and correct our behavior.

➢ When we are able to share our feelings and thoughts with our partner.

➢ When we are willing to listen to our partner's point of view without interrupting.

➢ When we love ourselves and our partner.

➢ When we can allow ourselves to be vulnerable with our partner.

➢ When we take care of ourselves and see that our own basic needs are met.

➢ When we help our partner's needs to be met.

➢ When we give to our partner freely of our love and affection.

➢ When we handle conflicts and problems as they arise.

➢ When we and our partner are good friends as well as good lovers.

➢ When we commit ourselves to our partner and are willing to work on our relationship.

➢ When we are willing to work on our own inner conflicts if they should be interfering with our relationship.

➢ When we seek help if needed before it is too late.

I caution you from being discouraged if you cannot live up to all of the above perfectly and immediately. It may take time for these concepts to be fully integrated and become a part of you. The main thing is that you and your partner see yourselves as learning, growing individuals, rather than closed-off beings. At times, progress might seem slow, but even small amounts of progress should be considered successes. It is in this spirit that I now present my final guidelines and suggestions to you, along with my best wishes for much happiness, satisfaction, and fulfillment.

Final guidelines and
suggestions

Think of your partner as an individual and not as an extension of yourself.

)(

Encourage your partner to grow and fulfill himself or herself as an individual.

)(

Treat your partner as an equal, not like your parent or child.

)(

Share responsibility for household chores and for care of the children, especially when both partners work full-time.

)(

Let your partner know what you are feeling, what you want, what you think, and what you need.

)(

Encourage your partner to tell you what is going on with him or her and listen attentively without interrupting.

)(

Don't take your partner for granted. Your partner needs your love and affection.

)(

Avoid flirting with others in your partner's presence.

)(

Plan romantic interludes, occasional weekends away, and quiet walks together.

){

Give lovemaking a high priority. Learn what pleases and excites your partner and let him or her know what pleases you.

){

Be authentic with your partner and avoid game playing. Allow yourself to be open and vulnerable with the person you have chosen to spend your life with.

){

Enjoy the present and make the most of each day and each moment.

){

Avoid digging up the past, because this brings no satisfaction. Expend your energy on creating your life as you want it to be.

){

Think about what is really important to you. If a close, loving relationship is what you want, be willing to invest your time and energy into making it so.

){

Develop yourself as an individual. See yourself as a growing person who learns from your experiences.

){

Seek out satisfying activities and adventures that you and your partner can share and enjoy together.

){

Develop and surround yourself and your partner with a circle of friends who have positive attitudes and who share similar values and interests.

)(

Avoid criticizing your partner for small or minor things and give your partner the benefit of the doubt.

)(

Bring major irritants or complaints to your partner's attention using "I" messages.

)(

When disagreements occur, avoid name-calling, accusing, threatening, intimidating, pressuring, bullying, pushing, shoving, hitting, etc. These can destroy your relationship.

)(

Settle disagreements by give-and-take and compromise. This means you sometimes give in when something is really important to your partner, your partner sometimes gives in to you when something is very important to you, and both of you sometimes compromise to reach an agreement.

)(

Be willing to apologize and offer reassurance for the future. Then keep your word. Integrity is your most valuable virtue.

)(

Should a major rift or problem develop that you and your partner cannot resolve, seek professional help.

Index

}215{

Printed in the United States
47737LVS00001B/247-318